Little O

Little O

DISCARD

BY EDITH UNNERSTAD

Illustrated by Louis Slobodkin

The Macmillan Company, New York

© THE MACMILLAN COMPANY 1957

All rights reserved. No part of this book may be repro-
duced or utilized in any form or by any means, electronic
or mechanical, including photocopying, recording or by
any information storage and retrieval system, without
permission in writing from the Publisher.

Original title: PIP-LARSSONS LILLA O
Translated from the Swedish by Inger Boye

Library of Congress catalog card number: 57-7269

PRINTED IN THE UNITED STATES OF AMERICA

SIXTH PRINTING, 1968

Elementary Library
Lake George Central School
Lake George, N. Y.

Contents

Little O

1. *Little O's Baby*

Little O was up in the attic with Mamma, who was putting away winter clothes in mothproof bags.

In a corner stood the old baby buggy Little O had used when she was a baby. She began pulling it back and forth in the small attic room. The rusty wheels creaked and screeched.

"Why does my nice buggy have to stay up here?" she asked: "Can't I have it downstairs in my room, Mamma?"

"What would you do with it there? You have your doll buggy."

"That's so small! I couldn't put a real baby in it. This one is much better. I could have Pysen in it and play that he was my baby brother."

"You and Pysen have so many things in your room," said Mamma. "And you'll soon get tired of it. Then I'll have to carry it up again."

"I won't get tired of it. I am going to play with it every day. I have never pulled a real baby buggy," complained Little O. "Please Mamma, can't I have my own buggy?"

"My goodness, how you carry on," said Mamma. "Well, I suppose we can bring it down for a few days anyway."

"Oh, goody," cried Little O. "I am going to make a nice bed in it, and then Pysen will like to ride in it."

"Think so?" said Mamma. "Well, here is the mattress that goes with it, and I have saved your little pink cover. I think it is in that box over there. Wait, we'll see—yes, here we have it."

"Pillow, too," said Little O. "And then we must have sheets with lace on them."

"Your small sheets for the buggy are downstairs, someplace. All right then, I'll carry the buggy down."

Little O helped Mamma carry the buggy down the stairs. That is, she tripped alongside, holding on to the handle. Mamma dusted off the buggy and said: "This buggy has been a faithful servant. All seven of you have used it, but there isn't much left of it now, I see. When you have finished playing with it, I think we shall put it beside the garbage can, so the man can take it away with the garbage."

"Oh no, please! It is so nice," said Little O. "There are almost no holes in the hood."

She made the bed with the old yellowed sheets and lace-decorated pillow cases, which she herself had used when she lay in the buggy. Carefully she smoothed out the wrinkles in the flowery pink cover, and opened up the worn hood. Then she began pushing the buggy around the house.

"Now, if only I had a rattle to hang on a string, so Pysen would have something to play with when he is lying there being a baby," she said.

"If you can get him to do it," said Mamma. "And *if* he can get into the buggy."

"He can squeeze himself in there, can't he?" said Little O.

But all the old rattles had worn out and been thrown away a long time ago. So Little O hung up a small baby angel that had been tied to a lollipop.

Mamma went up to the attic again, and Little O waited impatiently for Pysen to come home. He had gone with Papa to the shop.

And when he finally arrived, it was just as Mamma had expected. He didn't even want to hear about getting in the baby buggy.

"Get in there yourself, you are little enough," he said. "Say, Knutte and I could make a fine car from this old buggy. Pelle-Göran made one from their old one. If we just take off the hood, and put in a wheel . . . We can make a steering wheel from another wheel, if we can find one. Just wait, this is going to be a neat car."

"You are not going to take apart my nice buggy and make an old car out of it," said Little O, snatching away the buggy.

"But it isn't yours. I had it before you," said Pysen.

"Yes, but then I got it, and I had it last," said Little O. "And I am going to have it to wheel babies in. Mamma said I could. Please Pysen lie down in the buggy. Look what a nice bed I have made for you!"

"No—No! That's only for girls who like to play Mamma and children," said Pysen in a determined voice.

"No, not Mamma and children," said Little O. "You are going to be my little brother."

"Little brother!" exclaimed Pysen, "I am almost two years older than you. Don't try that! You can put your dolls in the buggy."

Little O began to cry.

"You are mean," she said. "It isn't any fun with the dolls. Because I want a little brother, that's what I want. You had me when I was little, but I haven't anybody. It isn't ri-hi-ght."

"Stop sniffling," said Pysen. "Baby brothers and baby sisters. Is that anything to have? Things that only cry and scream? Ugh!"

"You *liked* me when I was little," cried Little O, "you *did*, 'cause Mamma has said so. You often came and wanted to kiss me on the cheek, I know that."

"I don't think I did," muttered Pysen embarrassed.

But Little O continued: "Little brothers and sisters are terribly nice. Everybody has little brothers and sisters. But I don't. And I am not going out with the dolls. I have done that so often, almost every day. And the dolls don't fit in this buggy. They are too small."

"Take Sotarn, then," said Pysen. "And stop sniffling, I said."

"I am not sniffling," cried Little O.

With a final sobbing sound she stopped. Sotarn? She looked at the black cat lying in the window squinting against the sun through narrow, yellow slits. Wonder if . . . Well, if she couldn't get Pysen in the buggy, Sotarn would be better than the dolls anyway. At least he was alive. She *could* pretend that he was a baby.

But then she'd have to see to it that he became a little more like a baby brother. Baby brothers wear clothes. She pondered a bit, and then she figured it out.

In the old chest of drawers in the bedroom, she knew there was just what she wanted: the long, white christening dress all the Larsson children had worn when they were christened.

When Pysen saw that she had given up wanting him to be a baby in the buggy, he became more helpful and pulled out the heavy drawer for her. Then he held the struggling cat while she dressed him. It wasn't easy, because Sortarn didn't in the least want to join in all this nonsense. Once he broke away from them and dashed across the floor, the long dress trailing behind and one puffed sleeve on his back. It looked terribly funny, the way he stumbled and turned somersaults while biting and tearing at the nice dress trying to get out of it.

"Why don't you want to get dressed up, you little dummy?" said Little O.

Warm and tired, they finally got the dress properly buttoned and the silk ribbons on the bonnet tied under the small chin of the cat.

Poor Sotarn looked very unhappy, turning and twisting, trying to get out of all the finery, but when Little O put him down in the buggy and tucked him in, he became quiet, and made himself comfortable. He even slept a little.

"And now we shall go for a walk," said Little O.

Pysen helped her down the stairs with the buggy. Sotarn sat up and tried to jump out, for the buggy was shaking with every step. But when they were down in the yard finally, he became quiet again.

"O.K. Now you'll have to take care of yourself and your cat, because I am going over to Pelle-Göran's house," said Pysen and walked out through the gate.

Little O wheeled the buggy around the yard several times. Once in a while she would stop and busy herself with her new little brother, tucking him in a little better, jingling the baby angel, babbling and chattering.

"Now, you must be good, little one, and when we get home Big O will give you something very good. No, shame on you. Down with those itsy, bitsy hands, so they don't get cold. That's right. And don't pull them out again."

Then she sat down on a bench near the laundry and pushed the buggy slowly back and forth, the way she had seen mothers and nurses do in the park. She looked up at the row of windows, wishing that somebody might see and hear her, and wishing that they would think she actually had a little child in the buggy. But nobody appeared at the windows, and she decided to take the buggy out on the street instead. She pulled up the sheet so that only a bit of the lace bonnet showed. Then she steered the buggy out through the gate.

"No, baby, don't touch the sheet. Here on the street the wind will blow so cold, so cold on the little baby," she was chatting.

She hadn't walked very far before she met a gentleman and a lady, walking arm in arm. She looked up at them and smiled as much as to say: "Here I am wheeling my little brother!" But the two had so much to talk about that they didn't even notice the little carriage. Then came a gentleman reading a newspaper. When people are reading newspapers, they neither hear nor see, Mamma used to say, and that was true this time, too.

But then along came an elderly lady. Even from a distance Little O could see she was smiling delightedly.

"Such a good little girl you are, out wheeling your . . . it is a boy or a girl?"

"A boy," said Little O, smiling at her.

"So nice. And you are helping Mamma taking care of him. You like your little brother, don't you?"

"Awfully much," said Little O, giggling a little.

Just imagine, the lady thought, . . .

"And how old is he?" asked the lady.

"Three years old," said Little O, because she knew, that was how old Sotarn was.

"Three years old. No, that can't be possible," said the lady. "You mean three months old, don't you? My, oh my," she said, bending over the buggy. "May I take a look at the little baby?"

"Yes, but don't touch, because then he'll wake up," said Little O.

The lady stuck her curious face in under the hood. Just then Sotarn raised his coal-black, mustache-decorated head out from under the lace ruffles of the bonnet. He stared with yellow eyes at her, and then he yawned widely and rudely.

The lady let out a scream and leapt backwards. The little angel on the string caught in her hat, loosened from the hood and hung, dangling merrily over her ear.

"My goodness, what kind of a monster do you have in that buggy?" she screamed, gasping for breath. "My, how you scared me!"

Afraid of a cat!

"Haven't you ever seen a cat before?" said Little O surprised.

LOUIS SLOBODKIN

"A cat!" said the lady. "In a baby buggy! And dressed up!"

She picked the angel off her hat and let it fall down in the buggy as if she were afraid of it, too.

"Thank you," said Little O and curtsied.

The lady muttered something about, "what children can think of and yet be looking so sweet and good." She shook her head as she disappeared into the grocery store.

Little O tucked in Sotarn again and walked on. But the cat was restless. He didn't like to lie with his head down and feet up, and that's what he was doing just then, because they were going downhill. He crawled out time and again, miaowing anxiously. Little O scolded him.

"Shame on you, baby! If baby doesn't stay quietly in the buggy, Big O might never take you out again. Now there, play with your angel, baby, and be a little darling, and I'll give you a banana and some orange juice when we get home."

Then something happened.

A big police dog came trotting down the hill. Little O was walking with her back to him, otherwise she might have seen him in time. But as it was she only walked along, chatting soothingly, trying to calm the unhappy cat.

"Children are bothersome," she sighed after having put down Sotarn for at least the fifteenth time.

The police dog had almost reached them. He stopped, sniffing the air. The faint scent of cat which he had felt all along the sidewalk suddenly became much stronger. And just as Sotarn, for perhaps the sixteenth time, succeeded in getting his head over the side of the buggy, the dog and cat caught sight of each other.

What a hullabaloo! The dog tore furiously at the buggy, throwing his big paws over it. The buggy tipped and the cat slid forward. Arching his back under the white dress he stood up, spitting and furious. Little O screamed and struck at the dog, and in the confusion she let go of the buggy. It immediately took off on its own, and rolled down the hill, bouncing and with all wheels screeching. Barking loudly the dog pursued it. It sounded like three savage dogs, all yelping at the same time. Sobbing wildly, Little O raced after it as fast as her small legs would carry her.

People walking along the street looked in horror

at the lurching, runaway baby buggy. They saw the furious, yelping dog running after it, and the sobbing little girl. They all dashed up wanting to help. In bewilderment they called to each other: "The child! There is a child in the buggy. It might be killed if the buggy turns over. That dog looks mad. Catch him! We have to save the child."

"Sotarn! Dear little Sotarn! And my nice buggy," howled Little O in despair.

Just as the careening baby buggy reached a side street, a truck appeared. There was a sound of screeching brakes, then a loud bang. The buggy flew to one side and turned over. The onlookers held their breaths. One lady threw her hands over her face, crying: "The child, the poor child, I don't dare look to see what's happened to the child."

With the collision, Sotarn was thrown clear of the buggy. And now the startled spectators saw the poor run-over child in the gutter get up, shake itself and then take off up the hill on all fours, stumbling in the long, trailing dress. They could not believe their eyes. They just stood and stared, completely baffled.

"Wha-what is that—what in the world?" . . .

Close upon the heels of the runaway came the dog. And in a flash, he caught it. But it was only a strip of cloth from the christening dress that he got. The cat whirled around and with his sharp claws gave him a tearing slash on the ear. The dog howled. Again the cat tried to escape. But he got himself so tangled up in the dress he couldn't go very far. The dog followed.

By now Little O had reached them. And just as the big police dog was going to give her little brother a final blow on the neck, she flung herself on him, pushing him away.

"You bad thing!" she screamed, beating him with her clenched fists. "Let go of my cat, or I'll get you."

For a moment the dog was taken by surprise. Then, before he realized what was happening, Sotarn, in his torn christening dress with the lace bonnet hanging on his back, succeeded in scrambling through the open door of the fish market behind him.

Here an excited, laughing crowd soon gathered around Little O and her cat. The police dog stood outside the closed door, yelping and howling until he heard somebody whistle from the top of the hill. Then he slunk home.

Sotarn was angry. He kept up a steady muffled

growling the whole time that Little O was taking off the tattered, dirty dress and bonnet. And even when he became a cat again and no longer a dressed-up little brother, his ears still were lying back angrily. No wonder, the way he had been treated!

"Nice kitty," said the driver of the truck that had collided with the baby buggy. "And such a nice girl, too! Say, you're the youngest one of the Larsson's, aren't you?"

"Yes, we don't have any smaller ones," said Little O.

"You sure weren't afraid of tackling that big dog," said the driver.

"To think that she dared," cried the others, "and such a terrible dog he was, too."

"Oh, it's only Pompe in sixty-eight," said Little O. "He is just a coward, that's what he is. He only chases cats."

"Do you think your kitty would like some herring," asked the driver.

"That's what he loves most," said Little O.

The driver took out his big wallet. "Lady, may we have a kilo of herring for a fine kitty," he said.

While the fish lady weighed the herring, one of

the women held up the sad remnants of the Larsson children's christening dress.

"This must have been a very nice dress," she said. "Look, such fine embroidery. What do you think your Mamma will say when she sees it now?"

"And the baby buggy, too," said the driver. "That's completely smashed."

"It doesn't matter," said Little O. "We aren't going to have any more children, anyway. Little brothers and sisters are such a bother. Come on, Sotarn! Let's go home!"

2. *A Porcupine*

One day when it was "staying-inside" weather and Little O didn't know what to do with herself, Mamma taught her to braid.

She had a hank of mercerized cotton to practice on.

Her small fingers twisted and turned, imitating Mamma's as well as they could. The tip of her tongue crept out between her lips, twisting and working just like her fingers.

She made mistakes and sighed.

"It's so hard," she said when she lost her hold and the braid loosened.

"But it's lots of fun, too," she said a little later, sighing with relief. For then the braid finally was finished, and straight, too, although a bit uneven, of course. But she kept on with it, braiding and taking it up, braiding and taking it up again, and by and by she became quite good at it, and was able to braid both quickly and firmly.

"When I get to be a Mamma and have children, they are all going to have long braids and I shall fix their braids every day," she said.

"Then it would be best if you braided in a ribbon and tied a neat bow, otherwise it won't stay," said Mamma.

"Oh, then I can use my nice ribbons," said Little O and went to get her box of ribbons.

Little O collected silk ribbons and had one hundred and thirteen of them.

There were ribbons which had been on candy boxes and around nice Christmas presents. There were Mirre's hair ribbons from the time she wore long braids, and grosgrain ribbons from Rosalinda's hats. There were long ribbons and short ones, narrow ones and wide ones. Not only the family, but the whole apartment house saved silk ribbons for Little O. Old Miss Breemer had given her some narrow pink and light blue ribbons of the kind used to thread through small holes on embroidered underwear some years ago.

Aunt Bella had given her the box. It was covered with cretonne and had a bouquet of roses on the lid. And once when Aunt Bella had had some spare time, she had washed and ironed the ribbons and had helped Little O roll them up smoothly and nicely. The very finest ones didn't need to be washed. They were gold and silver ribbons, which had been on flower baskets Mamma had received on her birthdays.

So Little O learned to braid ribbons into braids and to tie neat bows. That was even harder than plain braiding. For it was so easy to get a hard knot or else the knot became too loose and the ribbon slipped off. But every time she did it, it became easier.

When Mirre came home from school, she had to be guinea pig. What's the use of learning to braid if one doesn't have real hair to braid? If only Mirre had long braids, of course, it would have been even more fun. But, anyway, that couldn't be helped.

Little O combed and braided. At each ear Mirre got a short, thick little pigtail decorated with a red bow from a Christmas package. Little O was delighted with her work and clapped her hands.

"Why, I have horns. I look like a cow," said Mirre when she looked at herself in the mirror.

Next came Rosalinda. But her hair was so curly it snarled. It was hard to get straight enough for braiding. Little O struggled and pulled, and the teeth in the comb were bending.

"Ouch," cried Rosalinda. "Don't pull like that."

Little O tried again. A new "ouch" followed.

"What a racket you make," said Lasse. "Do you have to yell like that for a little pull, big as you are!"

"She is pulling so hard she is tearing out my hair," grumbled Rosalinda. "Anyway, I don't have time for this. I am going out tonight, and I have to iron a blouse first."

She rose and went in the kitchen. A crestfallen Little O was left standing with all her beautiful ribbons.

Lasse suggested she braid the hair of her dolls. So Little O went after them. But Pysen had scalped Gullbritt once when they were playing Indians.

"And look at Malena's hair," said Little O. "Hers is so tangled you can't braid it. You can't even comb it. It just falls out. Whose hair can I braid? Dessi isn't home, and Mamma is too busy."

"Listen Mirre, can't you loosen your hair and let her do it again?" said Lasse.

"No thank you, once is enough," said Mirre.

"You aren't very nice to your little sister," said Lasse, "when she wants to do it so badly" . . .

"Let her braid *your* hair if that's the way you feel," said Mirre. "You have a big head of hair, at least over your forehead. It will do. I am going in to study."

Little O looked at Lasse with big sad eyes. Then they began to shine.

"Lasse! Could I, oh Lasse, could I? I will use my very nicest ribbons. And I promise not to pull."

"No, I should say not," said Lasse. "Boys don't braid their hair. How would I look? And bows, too. Never heard anything like it. No, little lady."

"O-o-oh," begged Little O. "That doesn't matter. It will be so nice, I promise. Only a tiny, little braid."

Lasse looked at her eager little face and somehow he weakened.

"Well, you can try, anyway," he said. "But I don't think you can get enough for a braid out of my hair."

"Oh yes, just wait and see," said Little O confidently.

Lasse stretched out on the sofa and Little O placed herself close to his head.

Little O combed his hair with a comb missing two teeth and began braiding it.

"Am I hurting you?" she asked anxiously.

"Not a bit," said Lasse patiently.

"Oh, Lasse you should see how nice it is, you won't believe it. And you shall have my shiniest gold ribbon if only you will lay still," she coaxed.

Lasse laughed and hummed:

> "And never came the suitor there,
> Before that second year,
> With golden ribbon in his hair."

"Well, there you see, boys can have golden ribbons in their hair after all," said Little O, braiding in the ribbon and tying a bow.

Lasse closed his eyes and let her go on, although he felt her making more than one braid. But, what did it matter. Little O might just as well have some fun. It didn't feel so good, though, the way she pulled his short hair.

Lasse had other things to think about, and he might just as well do that lying down as sitting up, trying to read. Should he invite a certain person to go to the movies with him on Saturday, even though he hardly knew her? Perhaps it was a little early since he had met her only once, and then only for a short time? And would it be all right to go and get something to eat afterwards? And how could he ask her without Rosalinda knowing about it? Wonder if he couldn't just call her up?

"Are you sleeping?" whispered Little O.

"Not quite," yawned Lasse.

"Want me to sing a little for you?"

"Mmm, you do that."

Little O sang, "Sleep you little pussy willow," while she worked. She finished one short little pigtail after the other, and tied all the ribbons into dainty bows.

Finally Lasse had a halo of stiff little pigtails around his forehead. They were standing straight out, each one ending in a bright bow of gold or silver.

The door bell rang and they heard Rosalinda go and open the door.

"Hi," she said. "Come right in and wait here. I am only going to change my blouse, and I'll be ready in a jiffy."

Startled out of his dreams Lasse jumped up, scattering the rest of Little O's ribbon collection all over the floor. He stared at the two girls who walked in. One of them was only old friendly Nottan, Rosalinda's best friend. But the other one—the other one was a certain person, just the one he had he had been thinking of inviting to a movie. Her name was Agneta, and she was new in Rosalinda's class.

Their entrance was so unexpected, he could barely greet them. He felt completely trapped.

"Hi," said the girls.

"Hi," answered Little O.

"But Lasse," cried Nottan, looking at him with big eyes. "How funny you look. WHAT do you have in your hair?"

"Curlers," giggled Agneta. "Well, I did think you had awfully curly hair. So that's why . . ." She teased.

Lasse was furious. He pulled and tore at the stiff little pigtails and the gay bows. But they weren't easy to loosen, especially with the girls standing there laughing and chattering.

"Take it off," he hissed at Little O. "She is learning to braid, you see. Now, get these darn things off."

Little O did what she could, but didn't get very far.

"They won't come off," she said worriedly. "There are hard knots on all the ribbons."

"Oh fine," fumed Lasse, fumbling angrily with the braids.

Between spells of laughter, Nottan and Agneta offered to help, but received only grunts for answers.

"You've got to look at yourself in the mirror before you get rid of your fine hair ribbons. You have no idea how fantastically funny you look," shrieked Nottan.

But who wants to look funny in front of a girl one sort of likes?

The bows dingled and dangled as Lasse tore at them. He got one off, but there were at least six or seven left.

"Scissors," he roared to Little O. "Believe me,

I am going to cut off every strand of hair, so I can get rid of this mess. Get me a pair of scissors, right away."

"You can't cut my pretty ribbons," said Little O frightened.

"Are you crazy?" cried Nottan. "Your nice hair. Wait I'll help you."

"I don't want any help," cried Lasse angrily.

Then he happened to glance at Agneta. "Don't you have any sense of humor at all?" her eyes seemed to say.

He went over to the mirror. It was even worse than he had imagined. He didn't look sane at all. No wonder they had laughed so hard.

"Is this Lars Larsson?" he said, roaring with laughter. "I think it looks like a porcupine decorated like a Christmas tree. Well, that's what one gets for being helpful to little sisters."

While Agneta and Nottan carefully freed him from the wonderful hair decorations, Little O picked up her silk ribbons and put them back in the box. Then she carried them down to the stable, and though she heard her brothers and sisters calling her, she stayed there until quite late in the evening. She was peeved at all of them.

She braided the manes and the tails of Laban and Lotta.

"You are nice, both of you," she said. "You like to be pretty."

They didn't struggle against her, only stared at her once in a while with their nice brown eyes.

The next morning when Lundkvist from the shop came to hitch up the horses, he couldn't believe his own eyes.

"Well, now what!"

Then Papa came to tell Lundkvist where to drive and what to get.

"What in the world does this mean?" he asked bewildered.

"Yes, tell me," said Lundkvist. "It's like a circus. See how those poor animals have been fixed. At the back and in the front, too."

"Little O must have been here," said Papa, amused. "But how could she do so many braids?"

Lundkvist started counting aloud. Laban had twenty-six braids, seven of them on his tail. Papa was just about to count the braids on Lotta's tail, when she turned her head and swished her tail. The braids lashed Papa across the face in a rather rough caress, and his glasses fell down on the stable floor.

Lotta whinnied gaily—it sounded like a pleased chuckle. And old Miss Breemer's lingerie bows dangled brightly around her ears.

"Well! Horses," said Papa.

"And kids!" said Lundkvist.

Little O's braiding disease, as they called it at home, lasted through the whole spring. She braided string, and fringes on carpets, table clothes, a traveling blanket and Mamma's best shawl. She even tried to braid her own fingers, although that didn't work so well.

But it was no use now to ask any of her brothers or sisters if she might braid their hair. Everybody sneaked away. And Lundkvist from the shop carefully kept the doors to the stable locked. So she couldn't get at Laban and Lotta either.

"It's a good thing to be bald," said Papa.

There was only one person whose hair she could braid as often as she wanted: one who had begun dropping in quite frequently, one who would say: "You may braid my hair tonight, if you want to." And that was Agneta, Rosalinda's classmate, whom Lasse took to the movies once in a while.

"She is so *terribly* nice," said Little O.

3.   *Tvaga and Benjibony*

Little O was in the bath tub. And when she took a bath, she really took a bath. She was a little savage in the bathroom, splashing, laughing and jumping around. Poor Dessi who was helping her was nearly drenched.

"That child will be the death of me," panted Dessi, closing the door to the bathroom. "I hardly have anything dry on."

Lasse looked up from the newspaper.

"Listen Dessi," he said eagerly, "here is something the two of us might try."

"I'll be there in a minute," said Dessi, "I'm putting some dry clothes on."

She took off her wet robe, changed into a dress and dried her hair.

Then she picked up her sketch book and returned to the living room.

"Best to get her when she comes out," she said. "I want to sketch Little O in this gay mood, just the way she is when she takes a bath."

"Well, you see, Dessi," began Lasse, "here in the newspaper . . ."

He didn't get any further. The door to the bathroom flew open, and Little O came rushing out, her moist hair standing on end, her cheeks rosy from the heat and her eyes sparkling mischievously.

"Oh, how nice it is to be clean," she sang, dancing and skipping around the room in her bare feet. The bathrobe fluttered around her, and the bathrobe cord dangled like a long tail behind her.

"Well, now about this contest, don't you think," began Lasse again.

But Dessi was busy with pad and pencil.

"Wait a moment," she said.—"Listen, Little O, keep it up for a while."

Little O happily continued her frolicking. She, like her brothers and sisters, was so used to sitting, standing and jumping while Dessi was drawing, that she hardly gave it a thought.

Lasse was laughing at her.

"You look like a cat chasing its tail," he said.

"With that tail I think she looks like a troll," said Dessi.

"I *am* a troll," panted Little O. "Don't you see I am a troll! Please, Dessi, draw me as a troll."

"That's what I am doing," said Dessi. "You have no idea how pretty you are going to be. Turn a somersault, but do it slowly, little Jumping Jack. That's it! That's fine. Now, once more."

"What is my name?" asked Little O, standing on her head. "I must have a troll name."

"Ask Lasse," said Dessi. "He is good at names."

"Find me a troll name, Lasse."

"Your name is . . . wait a moment . . . yes, your name is troll Tvaga. That's a good troll name, isn't it? And you are living behind the bath tub with your Papa and your Mamma and all your seven brothers and sisters."

"More," begged Little O. "Tell some more, Lasse."

Lasse peeked over Dessi's shoulder.

"Oh, fine," he said and laughed. "That is good."

Dessi sighed a little, and held up the drawing, looking at it critically.

"Well, yes, it isn't too bad. Now, what was it you wanted?"

"Oh, yes, listen to this," said Lasse. "There is a notice here about a contest for a story with illustrations. Look here! I saw it once before and thought about it then, but somehow I didn't do anything about it. Now, here is a reminder of the contest, saying there is just a month left. What do you say, shall we try for it? You draw and I write?"

"About me," cried Little O, clapping her hands. "About the troll Tvaga who lives under the bath tub."

Lasse and Dessi looked at each other.

"Should we?" said Dessi hesitatingly.

"Absolutely!" said Lasse. "I am going to start right away."

"On one condition," said Dessi. "Nobody else must know about it. We won't get any prize, of course. But it is so annoying if the whole family knows about it, and goes around imagining that we will be the winners and then later on pities us and feels sorry for us. Remember it is a secret, Little O, and don't go tattling to the others, understand?"

"I never tattle," said Little O, peeved, wrinkling her little nose.

"Don't disturb me now," said Lasse. "This is not going to be one of those ordinary troll tales, oh no. This is going to be something special."

Dessi went for her India ink, and Lasse got Papa's typewriter.

They worked all evening.

Lasse would write, then he would sit and think and tear his hair, and then he would write again. Once in a while he would chuckle a little, and Little O knew that he had thought of something funny. As soon as he finished one sheet he gave it to Dessi. She read it and laughed out loud.

"You are in fine form," she said.

"Read it to me," said Little O curiously.

"Not before the story is finished," said Lasse.

"Turn cartwheels for a while, Little O," said Dessi.

So Little O turned cartwheels and Dessi drew her.

"It says here that the bathroom trolls live on soap and pumice stone," said Dessi. "You may take an apple and munch on it, because I don't think you will like soap."

Little O munched her apple and Dessi sketched her.

"Isn't it lucky that the others are away tonight," mumbled Lasse, writing furiously, "otherwise Little O couldn't have stayed up this long."

At nine-thirty the story was finished. Lasse carried Little O in to bed, while Dessi drew the last strokes on the last drawing. Lasse had just finished reading the story to Little O, and Little O had just finished laughing when they heard Papa's deep voice, and Rosalinda's chatter on the stairway.

"Oh, if only we could get that prize," whispered Little O.

"We'll get it. Of course we will get it with those funny drawings Dessi has made," said Lasse.

"Sh-sh," said Dessi. "They are coming."

Little O soon forgot the whole thing. She had so much else to think about, to play with Pysen, visit Laban and Lotta in the stable, help Mamma bake, wipe the dishes and go shopping with her.

And the time passed.

One day she overheard Dessi saying: "It's the fourteenth today. Wasn't it tomorrow they were going to decide about that contest?"

"Yes," said Lasse. "Exciting, isn't it?"

"Oh well," said Dessi. "We don't have any chance, of course. But I hope they will return my pictures, anyway, because I could use them for Christmas cards. Listen, Little O, you will have to watch the mailman! If a big envelop comes for me —this big—bring it to me right away, wherever I am, so nobody else sees it, understand?"

"Even if you are in the bathroom?" asked Little O, "or downstairs in the yard?"

"Wherever I am," repeated Dessi. "And if you can't find me, give it to Lasse."

"I'll do that," said Little O, feeling very proud to be trusted with such an important task.

And she did watch. As soon as she heard a sound from the mailbox, she rushed out and picked up the mail. But it was always just newspapers or the usual small letters and cards, and disappointed she went inside again.

But one morning a big brown envelop fell down into the mailbox, exactly big enough for Dessi's pictures and Lasse's story. Yes, it was just like the envelop they had sent to the contest.

Lasse and Dessi were both in school, and Little O herself was all dressed to go out in the yard where Pysen and Pelle-Göran from thirty-nine were learning to ride bicycles.

Dessi had asked her to bring the big envelop to her right away, no matter where she was. And now she had gone to school. Little O knew where Dessi's and Lasse's school was. It was not far away.

She grabbed the big envelop, and started off.

Right away, Dessi had said. That meant she had to be very quick about it. She slid down the stairs and hurried out through the gate as fast as she could.

Not until she was out in the street did she happen to think that she wasn't exactly dressed for going to school. The coat and the pants which she wore for playing were patched and too small. They were supposed to be used only in bad weather, and only in her own yard. And she had on the kitty-beret, the one Mamma had said was ready for the garbage can a long time ago. The kitty-beret was a faded blue angora cap. Little O liked it because it was so soft and fluffy. Of course, it didn't look very nice any more. It had a stain from a newly painted spout, and had become rather ragged. But Little O had worn it often without Mamma knowing it.

Should she go back now and change? But Dessi had said: right away! And if she went up again, perhaps Mamma would see the envelop which no one but Dessi or Lasse was supposed to see. No, she had better go on.

She ran and she ran. Soon she stood panting outside the school. The yard was empty, and in a little pool of water in front of the stairs, two small sparrows were taking a bath. Little O laughed when she saw how they shook themselves, sprinkling their feathers. Then she began climbing the stairs.

Inside there were stairs and stairs, and doors and doors. She opened one door a little and peeked in. She saw only a crowd of small boys. They were much bigger than she, of course, but much smaller than Lasse. They turned and looked at her in surprise.

Why did they stare like that? Oh, it must be that kitty-beret. Maybe they thought she was strange, coming to school dressed in her play clothes. And none of the boys wore caps. Maybe they weren't allowed to wear caps in school. Quickly she closed the door and hurried away. In another corridor she noticed a number of coats hanging on the wall, and caps up on the shelf above. Should she put hers there? But that old kitty-beret wasn't nice enough to put on a shelf for school caps. And besides, she couldn't reach the shelf.

Now she heard footsteps. It sounded as if someone was coming up the stairs. And here she stood with her old beret. Suppose it was a teacher who would say she couldn't go in and see Dessi if she had on her beret.

She had better hide it quickly. But where? She probably shouldn't put it on the floor, either.

The steps approached the corner where she stood, hesitating.

Little O opened another door, and this time she was in luck. There was nobody in there. She slid in quickly, closing the door behind her.

But what was this? Did they have animals in school? A squirrel—yes, it surely was a squirrel. It sat there on a branch, staring at her with shiny, brown eyes. And everywhere on the shelves were birds, big ones and small ones, and on the window sill stood a cat, a speckled giant cat, ears tipped with tufts of hair.

"Puss, puss!" coaxed Little O, carefully walking nearer, because it was so big it almost looked dangerous.

Funny, it didn't move. The squirrel also sat still, and all the birds, too.

"Aren't you alive?" asked Little O. "Are you only toy animals, even if you are so big?"

It was strange, though, that Dessi and Lasse never had said a word about animals in the school.

Little O went over and cautiously touched the big cat. No, it wasn't alive, and it smelled of bad medicine which stung her nose. She tried pinching its stomach to see if it would make a noise like her own white toy cat. But its stomach was hard, and not a single little miaow would it make.

Walking around, she looked at the birds and the squirrel and some glass cases filled with beautiful butterflies. She thought it was a wonderful room, and would have liked to stay longer and play with the nice animals, if only she hadn't been in such a hurry to bring Dessi the brown envelop.

Where could she put her beret? In that closet, perhaps?

It was dark in the little room. And what was that

she saw in there? Not an animal, and it wasn't a man, either. Little O opened her eyes wide in amazement.

Maybe it was a man after all. A funny man of some kind, which someone had made. My, you could look through him. Straight through his strange, thin and bony body she could see rows of glass jars standing on shelves behind him, and he didn't have any hair on his bald, yellow head either. But no one had put in his eyes, even though holes were made for them. But teeth he had, and it looked as if he were smiling broadly. He wasn't nice, no! But maybe he would look better when finished.

"You poor thing without any hair," said Little O.

There was a stool in the closet. Little O climbed up and put the kitty-beret, a little crookedly, on the bare head.

"You look much nicer now!" she said. "And such fine teeth they have given you. They look exactly like real ones."

Then she picked up the brown envelop which she had put on the floor, and hurried out to find Dessi.

The halls were empty, and there was nobody to

ask. She went up one flight of stairs and peeked through a couple of doors. There were many boys, and in one room there were big girls, too, but none of them looked like Lasse or Dessi.

Through the third door came well-known sounds, making her feel good and also making her forget her errand. They were singing in there, and Little O loved singing.

She opened the door. About twenty or thirty boys stood singing, and way back in the room, close to the piano, stood a man keeping time with a little stick.

They were singing, "Roar like thunder, brothers." Little O knew the song and joined in. Of course, she ought to sing, when she knew the song. At home she always sang along as soon as someone began singing.

She sang as loudly as she could. She forgot Lasse and Dessi and the big brown envelop. She forgot that her jacket was too small and her pants had a big patch. Happily she stepped through the door, singing with the others. She didn't notice that several of the boys stopped singing, and she didn't hear the giggling and the scraping of feet. She was looking hard at the man who stood in front of her waving his arms, and sort of cutting the air to pieces with a stick.

> "Life and blood for Sweden's honor
> Swe-ar
> Faithful brothers hand in hand,"

she sang. She came in a little after the others, and her shrill peep, "hand in hand" rang out alone, after the boys had stopped.

The man with the stick lowered his arms.

"What was that?" he asked in surprise, opening his eyes, which he had kept closed during the song.

"It's only me," laughed Little O. "I can sing much more. I know so many songs."

"Oh, you do," said he, with a trace of a smile, while the boys snickered and shoved one another. "So-o. But what is on your mind now?"

Little O misunderstood him. She thought he was asking her what was her favorite song.

"Oh, there are several I like," she said. "I always go around singing."

"I think you would like to sing some of your songs for us, wouldn't you? Which one do you know, for instance. 'Ba, Ba, Black Sheep', perhaps?"

"Oh," said Little O, "that is so childish. I know one that is much better."

She could not understand why they were laughing so much.

Then Little O began. She sang loudly and clearly.

"San Borrombon, where dwells my sweet inamorata,
Lies not so far from busy Rio de la Plata
On the romantic
Beaches of the Atlantic
With the Pampas behind it in a hundred verdant miles;
There I come riding while the April moonlight smiles,
For I wish to dance the tango."

"Don't you know 'Carmencita?'" she said. "Why don't you sing instead of standing there laughing?"

Then they laughed even more, both the man with the stick and the boys. But almost all of them began singing, the man with the stick, too.

"Carmencita, little girl,
You have got me in a whirl!
I should like to tell your Papa and your Mamma
That I want to marry you, Carmencita."

They sang all the verses, and once in a while they made mistakes and didn't know the words. The man with the stick, didn't even know it as well as the others, so he sat down at the piano and played

"Carmencita," instead. Little O, with eyes shining, sang at the top of her voice and she knew all the words. It was so much fun, she actually had a ticklish feeling in her stomach.

When they finished with "Carmencita," Little O thought of starting with "Two little trolls living in a sieve," but suddenly she remembered the troll Tvaga and the envelope she had in her hand.

"Oh, oh," she said quickly. "I forgot. I must go and find Dessi right away."

"Who is that?" asked the man with the stick, "is it a girl? Is she in school here?"

"Of course," said Little O, "but I can't find her. There are so many doors in this school, and in almost all the rooms are boys."

"Is it your sister? And what is her name?"

When she said Larsson, somebody said: "Dessi Larsson, she is in L:4."

"Somebody take her there," said the man with the stick. "And thank you, dear Carmencita, for singing so nicely for us."

"You sang nicely, too," said Little O politely. "And I'll be going now. Good-bye to you all."

"Good-bye," they all called after her.

Just as she and the boy, who was taking her to

Dessi, got out in the hall, the bell rang for recess. Doors flew open, and boys came tumbling out from every direction. Then Lasse appeared!

"Little O," he said in alarm. "Why are you here? Is something wrong?"

"I came to give you this," she whispered, holding up the big envelope.

Lasse looked at the address.

"I don't understand," he said. "What do I want with that?"

Little O came close to him, for curious boys were pressing all around them.

"Don't you remember?" she whispered. "I can't find Dessi, and then I was supposed to give it to you, right away, 'cause that's what Dessi said, so I had to come to school, don't you see?"

Lasse whistled, and then he began to laugh.

"What's the matter? Why are you laughing?" said Little O. "Wasn't it good that I came?"

"Of course, Little O, it really was smart of you to come," said Lasse. "It's only that this is not for Dessi and me. It is a letter for Papa from the patent office. See here, it says Mr. P. I. P. Larsson."

"Oh-oh-oh," said Little O.

"You couldn't know that, of course, since you

can't read. But thank you anyway. And now I think you had better go home. Come, I'll take you to the gate."

"But I must get my kitty-beret," said Little O.

"Where did you leave it?"

"With that funny man."

"What funny man?"

"The one in the closet."

But she couldn't get Lasse to understand what she meant, and she had forgotten where the room was, so they had to look into several rooms before they found the right one.

"Here it was," she finally said, when she saw the squirrel and the giant cat.

"You have been in the zoology room, too?" said Lasse. "You sure can get around."

"Why is that cat so big?" asked Little O. "Do you think that Sotarn will get that big, too?"

"That is not a cat, it is only a cousin of the cat," said Lasse. "It is called a lynx. Now where is your kitty-beret?"

Little O opened the door to the closet.

"There," she said pointing.

Lasse didn't say a word. He just stood there and stared.

"What's the matter with you?" asked Little O. "Why do you look so funny?"

"Benjamin!" gulped Lasse. "Did you . . . no, that can't be true. Who put your beret on Benjamin Bony?"

"I did it, of course," said Little O. "I had to climb up on this stool. I thought his head might be cold because he hasn't any hair."

And she climbed up on the stool again and pulled the kitty-beret off the funny man.

"Was it really this that you were calling a funny man?" asked Lasse.

"Yes, because he isn't real. Look, he is laughing. He looks so funny. And I didn't know his name was Benjibony."

"What a kid," groaned Lasse, leaning against the bird cage. "Say, weren't you afraid of touching him?"

Little O looked at her brother with surprise. "Afraid of him? He isn't even alive," she said.

"Alive, no, that's just exactly what he is not," sputtered Lasse.

"Bye there, old Benjibony!" cried Little O as they left.

"Go home, now, with Papa's letter," said Lasse.

"And if more big envelopes come, don't bring them to school, just put them on my desk."

The schoolyard was filled with boys and girls. She didn't see Dessi, but near the gate stood a group she recognized.

"Look, here comes our Carmencita," one of them said.

Little O's cheeks blushed with delight, and she sang "Carmencita" loudly all the way home.

After she pushed the big envelope back into the Larsson mailbox, she went down to watch Pysen and Pelle-Göran from thirty-nine learning to ride a bicycle.

In the afternoon mail that same day, came a letter for Dessi and Lasse. It was not a big brown envelope, just a small white one. In it, it said that the charming and original story about Tvaga, and the drawings which showed great talent, had won the first prize of five hundred kronor in the contest.

"I can't believe it," said Dessi, who was so happy she cried.

Lasse felt so good he had to take a giant jump right up on the table, where he stood, yelling "Hurrah," again and again.

Elementary Library
Lake George Central School
Lake George, N. Y.

"Well, my goodness," said Mamma.

"Not bad, at all," said Papa.

"We're all right, Dessi. Both of us," cried Lasse. For Dessi had always dreamed about being an artist, and Lasse had always wanted to be an author.

"I am almost beginning to think so," said Dessi, her voice trembling. "At least there was a real professor of art among the judges for the contest."

"Just imagine, five hundred kronor," said Knutte.

"Little O is going to have a bit of it, too," said Lasse, "for she was our model."

"What are you going to buy with your money, Little O?" asked Pysen. "A car, maybe? Get a station wagon, so all of us can ride in it."

"Listen to that! There won't be enough money for a car," said Knutte.

"I know," said Little O. "I am going to buy myself a new kitty-beret, and then Benjibony can have my old one."

"What Benjibony? What do you mean?" asked Knutte.

Little O and Lasse looked at each other and laughed.

"Benjamin Bony, the school skeleton," said Lasse.

4. Truls and Pella

Little O was home alone. She had just had the measles. The spots were gone, and she was up again, but she couldn't go out yet. Pysen and Knutte were supposed to keep her company, for Mamma had gone to her sewing circle. But then came Pelle-Göran from thirty-nine, and asked if Pysen couldn't come over and play with him. So Pysen went over there. Later on Knutte had to go to the library with a book, and, of course, he was delayed there, so that's why Little O was all alone.

First she played with her dolls, then she drew pictures and looked at picture books. But she had done all that every day for a whole week, and it had become tiresome.

She padded out in the hall and opened all the umbrellas, pretending she was living in a tent. But to live alone in a tent wasn't fun, either. There ought to be two, at least, to do that, she thought. Too bad that none of the others were home. She could think of a thousand games to play with others, but not a single one to play all by herself.

Suddenly she noticed the telephone on the hall table. It wouldn't be such a bad thing to call up somebody and chat awhile. Then she wouldn't feel so all alone. But did she dare?

She had talked on the phone with Papa and Mamma and Aunt Bella many times. But somebody else had always called the number for her. She wasn't allowed to dial by herself, for Mama said she was too little. Of course, she didn't know the numbers yet. Well, she could count to twenty, but she didn't understand what was on the dial. Whenever she tried to call, Mamma or one of the others would come and take the receiver away from her.

"You call on your own phone," they would say.

That silly red toy telephone that didn't answer one word!

But the others were not at home now, so they couldn't tell her not to use the real telephone. That decided it.

She climbed up on a chair and lifted the receiver off the hook.

"Tut-tut-tut," it said in her ear.

She stuck her round little forefinger in a hole and began turning the dial. She knew how to use the telephone, even if the others didn't believe it.

It took a long time before anybody answered. She had to poke and turn many, many times. But suddenly she had it.

"Tut-tut," it sounded, and then she heard a lady's voice in her ear:

"58411," it said.

Little O was happy. See, she knew how to use the telephone.

"Hello, is this Aunt Bella?" she asked.

"The Svensson Brothers Hardware Store," said the voice.

"Oh," said Little O. "No thank you, I don't want any hardware today. Good-bye Hardware Store."

She put the receiver back, and after a while she tried again.

"Tut-tut-tut . . ."

But she didn't get anything. She twirled and she poked and put the receiver back again. And then she poked and turned again until her head ached from trying so hard. Just imagine it being so difficult to telephone.

When she was about to give up, it tut-tutted again. "Hello."

A deep voice answered. This certainly was Papa. Yes, of course, this must be Papa. Fine. Very good. Just think, she could call Papa, after all! She certainly was going to tell that to Pysen and Knutte when they came home.

"Hello to you," said Little O. "This is me."

"Oh, it is, and who is me?" wondered the voice.

"Papa," said Little O and laughed, "you are Papa, of course."

"Am I?" said the voice, laughing, too. "Are you sure? And who are you?"

Papa, that tease, he was always having fun.

"Don't you hear it is Little O?" she said. "Please Papa, can't you come home soon? Mamma has gone to the 'Sewing Sweater,' and it isn't any fun here."

She thought it was called "Sewing Sweater" because most of the ladies were knitting sweaters.

"Poor little thing," said the voice. "Don't you have anybody to play with?"

"No, they all have gone out. Please Papa, come home."

"You know, it is too bad," said the voice, "but I really am not your Papa."

And now it didn't sound as if he were teasing. And thinking it over, it didn't sound a bit like Papa, either.

"Oh," she said. "Is it Lundkvist from the shop then? Please Lundkvist, tell Papa I would like to talk to him."

"No, it really isn't Lundkvist, either," said the voice. This is 57685. What's your Papa's number?"

"Don't know," said Little O. "But can't *you* come over and play with me then?"

"Thank you, but I really haven't played for many years, so I don't think I would be very good at it," said the voice, chuckling a little.

Then it was silent for a moment, and Little O was wondering if she should say good-bye and hang up the receiver. But then the voice came back again, and this time it sounded both lively and teasing.

"Say, wait a moment," it said. "Perhaps, after all . . . Tell me, where do you live?"

"West St. Per's street, hundred and nineteen," said Little O.

That she knew. They had taught her that, so she wouldn't get lost.

"That's right here in the neighborhood," said the voice. "And what's your Papa's name?"

"His name is Per Ivar Patrick Larsson. And Mamma is called Maja Larsson. We are the P. I. P. Larssons."

"Ah, then I know. Well, how would you like it, if I came up and brought you some playmates?"

"Oh, please do," cried Little O. "Hurry and come right away."

"How many do you think I should bring?"

Little O thought that over. Perhaps it wouldn't be wise to invite too many when she couldn't ask Mamma first.

"Two," she said.

But then she remembered something.

"Have they had the measles?" she asked anxiously. "For otherwise I might give it to them,

Mamma said. But I am almost well now, I am up all day, and the day after tomorrow I can go out, that's what the doctor said."

The voice was really laughing now.

"You know, I don't think there is any danger of contagion with such playmates as these. No, you don't need to be afraid of that. Well, so long, then. We'll soon be over, all three of us."

Little O was so happy, she leaped from the chair, and sat down on the floor with a bang. She jumped up again and ran out in the kitchen to look in the cookie jar.

Yes, there were lots of cookies she could offer her guests. She was sure Mamma would let her do that. Mamma always offered cookies to all the children who came to play in the house.

And from the doll chest she took out the best doll clothes and dressed Gullbritt and Malena, so she wouldn't have to be ashamed of her children when her new playmates arrived.

Just as she finished, the bell rang. Little O rushed out and opened the door.

But what was this?

There stood a man with two small round puppies on a leash. One was pure white, the other one coal black, and both had soft brown eyes, small pink tongues and their coats were bushy and shining. Little O had never seen anything as happy as they were. They wagged their tails and stood on their hind legs, pulling at the leash and wanting to greet her.

"Oh," said Little O.

She thought that she had never seen anything so sweet.

"Good day to you, Little O," said their master. "Here we are. The black one is called Truls and the white one is Pella. They are very nice puppies, and nobody needs to be afraid of them. They are Samoyeds. And as you can see, they both are terribly anxious to come in and play with you for a while."

Little O was so happy she couldn't say a word. The puppies jumped up to lick her hands. Their master hung the leash on a hook in the hall, saying he didn't have time to stay, but that he would come back for Truls and Pella in a couple of hours.

That was some afternoon. How much fun Little O had! She and the puppies played hide-and-seek, tossed ball and had a tug of war with an old torn sock. The puppies growled and yapped, but only in fun, and Little O growled as well as she could, too.

They tore a newspaper into a thousand pieces and rolled around on the rug. They slid back and forth in the long hall until they were all three panting. Then Little O took the puppies into the kitchen where she fed them cookies and milk. She really spilled very little, besides, Truls and Pella licked it up, so there was hardly a sign of it.

She finally put them to bed in her doll buggy. The puppies were so tired after all that playing and all the food that they fell asleep at once, sleeping as soundly as if they were at home.

When Mamma returned from her sewing circle, Little O sat there singing: "Sleep you little pussy willow," to Truls and Pella. Mamma threw up her hands when she saw the woolly heads on the doll pillow.

"What in the world?" she said. "Where did they come from, those little darlings?"

"They are my playmates," said Little O proudly. "I called on the telephone, and then they came."

"You did *what*?" asked Mamma in amazement. "Did you telephone and order a couple of puppies? I never heard anything like it."

"Well, when you all left me," said Little O, "it wasn't any fun, and I didn't know what to do, so I

went out in the hall and called. And I could do it all by myself, Mamma. I really could!"

Mamma questioned her and questioned her. She could not understand how Truls and Pella had come to the house on West St. Per's street. Little O tried to explain, but it wasn't very easy.

After a while, however, the owner of the puppies came for them, and he told Mamma how it had happened. He said that his dog had seven puppies, and that he really didn't know what to do with all of them. So, if Mrs. Larsson had no objections, he would like to give a couple of them to Little O.

"Samoyeds are about the best dogs one can have for children," he said. "Strong and patient. One can play with them as much as one wishes, and they are never ill-tempered."

"Mamma," said Little O. "Can we, oh, can we?"

"Say please," Mamma said.

Just then the puppies woke up and started playing again. Mamma sat there, looking at them as they tumbled around.

"Well, I know it will be a lot of extra work. Anyway, I'll have to ask Papa what he says about it."

Just as she was saying that, Papa came home.

"What now? What does this mean?" he said surprised.

Little O threw herself around his neck. But she needn't have been worried. It was clear that Papa could not say no to Truls and Pella when he heard how it all had happened.

"Nobody can resist those two," he said.

Joyfully Little O jumped up and down. Then she hugged Mamma and Papa and the owner of the puppies, thanking them over and over again.

"You are very welcome," said the dog owner. "And now you don't have to feel lonesome when Mamma goes to her 'Sewing Sweater.'"

Mamma sighed and laughed at the same time.

"Well, I suppose we are a little crazy," she said. "Now we have two horses, a cat and two dogs, not to mention seven children."

"We ought to be grateful she didn't telephone for an elephant," said Papa.

"I can do that next time," said Little O.

"I wouldn't be surprised," said Mamma.

5. *The First Graduate*

Dessi was going to graduate from college. The whole family was excited. The first graduate at the Larssons! Suppose she didn't pass! Too often, perhaps, she had been hanging over her sketch book instead of studying hard like all her classmates.

"I have been a fool, but it is too late to study now. If I flunk, I flunk," said Dessi gloomily.

"I don't think you'll flunk," said Lasse. "You managed the written examinations, didn't you?"

"Yes, but it was a very close shave," said Dessi. "And the written ones aren't too bad. You have time to think with them. But for the oral ones you have to have the answers right away! I know it won't go well!"

"Can't you ask that Oral one to wait a little while?" said Little O, who thought this was some teacher, so called for fun.

Everybody laughed. Even Dessi smiled a little.

"I can't imagine anybody wanting to go to college," said Mirre.

Mirre was going to graduate from seventh grade this spring, and then, no more school for her. She never had liked to study. When summer came she was going to cook at a vacation camp, and in the fall she was thinking about working in a nursery school. No more studying than was necessary for her.

"Don't worry, Dessi," said Mamma. "We are all going to keep our fingers crossed for you, and then I am sure it will come out all right."

"I am going to keep my fingers crossed, too," piped up Little O. "On both hands, I promise."

"Thank you, little troll," said Dessi, smiling faintly.

"We are all going to come down to the schoolyard for you," said Pysen. "We are going to . . ."

"Sh," whispered the others. "You weren't supposed to say anything to her."

But Dessi wasn't so absent-minded she didn't understand.

"Can't you stop planning and getting things in order!" she said. "I know I am going to flunk, and then you'll be standing there with all the things you have been getting ready, while I have to sneak out the back door."

Papa joined in the conversation.

"It is true that there is a possibility that you may flunk," he said. "But if so, it isn't everything. How many painters and other artists do you think have graduated from college? And it is a painter you want to be, isn't it?"

"She *is* a painter," said Lasse.

"Dessi paints terribly nice," said Little O, lovingly patting the arm of her big sister.

"You'll see, it will come out all right," said Rosalinda, "and with that hair of yours, you'll look awfully nice in your graduation cap. I wish I had gone that far."

Her brothers and sisters all sounded so confident about it, much more confident than they really felt.

Little O was the only one who was absolutely sure that everything would turn out all right.

On the morning of the examination days she followed the nervous Dessi to the door where her brothers and sisters were waiting to give Dessi their good luck kicks.

"Don't you worry, Dessi! I am keeping my fingers crossed on both my hands. Look!"

She folded both her thumbs under her forefingers and closed her small fists.

And she kept her word. Not once did she let go. She kept her fingers crossed all day, until they hurt and felt numb. She refused to eat, because she couldn't hold a spoon with her fingers crossed. Mamma had to feed her. When she went out to play she met the mailman on the stairs, and showed him her crossed fingers. "Look mailman," she said, "Dessi is taking her exams."

"You are forgetting to keep your fingers crossed," she would say, first to Pysen, then to the others.

And it was true, for none of the others took this as seriously as Little O did. Once in a while they remembered and kept their fingers crossed a little while, but then they let go again.

The exams were supposed to be over around four o'clock. At three-thirty Lasse drove up with Laban and Lotta and the big saucepan journey wagon. It was newly painted and decorated with gay balloons. Up climbed all the Larssons, Aunt Bella and old Miss Breemer, who no longer used an earphone, just a small modern apparatus that looked like a button.

They were all carrying flowers, but Little O's bouquet of lilies of the valley was tied with a ribbon around her neck. And the beautiful red balloon which she, herself had chosen and which looked like a blown-up cat, was fastened in a button hole of her jacket. For when you have your fingers crossed, you can't hold on to anything else.

Then, off they went to the school. The grounds were crowded with people, balloons, flowers and all kinds of strange vehicles in which the students were going to ride. There were beautiful passenger cars and there were trucks, there were hayracks and a fine old-fashioned landau, there were carts of many kinds, even a wheelbarrow and a bicycle cart. And all were decorated with flowers and funny, painted posters. But even so, there was great excitement

when the Larssons arrived. The old saucepan sign had been painted over and there stood DESSI instead, in large letters. Many people there knew the family, and others had heard about it. So when the big Percheron horses came clumping in on the school grounds, people looked and said to each other: "There come the Larssons, and those are the horses, Laban and Lotta."

The horses had bunches of cowslips on their ears. Lotta, of course, saw fit to misbehave. First she ate up Laban's one bouquet. And when she could not get at the other one, she snorted and very annoyed, tried to sample the graduation flowers, which waiting relatives and friends were carrying. Fortunately Lasse had time to give a warning signal, and the people carrying the flowers moved away, with Lotta standing there, glaring at them.

But a short lady in a hat, decorated with violets, came within Lotta's reach for a moment. Flowers are flowers, perhaps Lotta was thinking, and nonchalantly snatching the pretty hat from the head of the owner, she began chewing it.

"My hat," cried the lady.

Papa Larsson rushed over to Lotta and rescued what was left of the veil and violets. But the hat didn't look exactly like a hat any more. Papa told the lady he was terribly sorry and said he would like to buy her a new hat.

But the lady just laughed and said: "Oh, forget it! What does a hat matter, if my boy passes his examinations today."

"Then, maybe I can have that pretty ribbon," said Little O to Rosalinda, pointing to the lavender velvet bow on the ruined hat.

And in so doing, she discovered to her distress that she had let go of the fingers she was keeping crossed for Dessi.

But now it didn't matter any longer. For at that same moment a window in the school was thrown open, and a voice called out: "Everybody has passed."

"Hurrah!" shouted Mirre, loud as a foghorn jumping up and down, feet close together. "She has passed! Dessi has passed!"

Mamma and the strange lady, whose hat Lotta had eaten, hugged one another, and then almost cried and then almost danced and almost behaved like little children, as Knutte said later on. But every one in the schoolyard was just as happy, and soon began grumbling: "Aren't they coming out?"

Finally the new graduates came out with Dessi among them. She looked very pale, so it must have been hard. After much kissing and hugging, Dessi and the other graduates were hoisted way up in the air, while people screamed "Hurrah, Hurrah," until they were almost deaf. And Dessi received so many flowers and balloons that she could hardly be seen from underneath them all.

Little O was so small she almost disappeared in the crowd. She squealed like a pig.

"Dessi," she called, "Dessi."

Papa got hold of her, hoisted her up on his shoulders and brought her over to Dessi. When Little O squeezed Dessi and gave her the bouquet of lilies of the valley, she whispered: "Now you see, you didn't flunk."

"Thank you, little darling," said Dessi.

When Dessi saw the saucepan wagon, she opened her eyes wide. She hugged Laban and Lotta and said that no one else had such a wonderful cart to ride in, and that it would be so much fun to ride in it once more in her life.

"You are not going to sit inside, you are going up on the top," said Lasse.

Both Dessi and Little O were lifted up on the

roof, and the girls and Knutte and several other boys and girls climbed up also. There they sat, dangling their feet, like a fringe of legs all around the top of the wagon. But Papa and Mamma, Aunt Bella and old Miss Breemer and some older persons went inside. Lasse and Pysen sat up on the driver's seat, and as they drove along, everybody sang the graduate's school song so loudly it echoed from house to house.

"Lasse, let us drive all around," said Dessi.

"Well, you don't think I am going to drive straight home, do you?" said Lasse.

Little O was sitting in the middle of the roof, near the sign with DESSI on. She sat between Dessi and a boy called Göran. He had graduated the year before, and was now in military service. He and Dessi were holding hands behind Little O's back. She knew it, of course, but she didn't let on at all. She helped Dessi by holding many of her flowers. Some of the bouquets were hanging from long blue and yellow silk ribbons, and stuck in some of them were tiny graduation caps.

"Can I have the ribbons?" she whispered to Dessi.

"Of course," said Dessi.

"And one of those doll caps, too?"

"Two, so you can play that Gullbritt and Malena have graduated."

"Oh, I am so happy," said Little O.

"Don't you think I am," said Dessi. "If you only knew . . ."

The window on the side of the cart was suddenly pushed open and Mamma stuck her head out.

"Little O isn't going to fall off is she?" she said anxiously.

Lasse stopped the horses, and climbed up on the seat to see how things were up there on the roof among all the flowers.

"No danger," he said to Mamma. "They are packed like a stew with vegetables all around, and Little O, a small royal sausage in the middle."

Then he clucked to Laban and Lotta, and the wagon rolled along the streets and the market places in Norrköping.

Little O looked at Dessi's white cap, at the flowers and the balloons, at the happy company around her on the roof of the wagon, and at the people down on the street, who stopped to laugh and wave at them. Then she looked down at her small fingers which still felt a little sore after having been imprisoned for such a long time.

Just think, that all these wonderful things really had happened because of her. What would have happened without Little O? She was the only one who had managed to keep her fingers crossed the whole day.

And while Laban and Lotta were jogging homeward to West St. Per's street with the old saucepan wagon, she sang with the others:

"Sing of the graduate's happiest day!
Let us rejoice in the spring of the youth."

6. *Itchy Fingers*

In the middle of June the family moved to the country.

Papa and Lasse and Lundkvist from the shop were building a new cottage close to Aunt Bella's old one, where they usually lived in the summer. Good Aunt Bella loved having them there but the cottage wasn't quite large enough now that the children were getting so big.

So Papa bought a lot from Miss Breemer, who

owned a large part of the ground along Blueviken. Her own big bungalow was called "The Reste," because it was built at a time when summer places were supposed to have peaceful names. "Fridhem," meaning home of peace, "Vilhelmsro," rest for William, and "Signesminne," in memory of Signe, were names for summer homes. Lasse had christened "The Reste," "Ye Reste," because of the old-fashioned spelling on the name plate. All the children, of course, called it "Ye Reste," just as he did. Aunt Bella's cottage, which also had belonged to Miss Breemer, was called "Lugnet," a place that is calm. However, the new cottage was going to be called "Oron," which means "Turmoil," for that was a name best suited to a house in which the Larssons lived.

Papa and the boys had completed enough of the cottage so Lasse and Knutte could use one of the rooms, but otherwise it was only half-finished. All day long they hammered and nailed. Knutte was assistant helper, and once in a while Pysen was allowed to help, also. But Papa preferred not having Little O around while they were building, for boards might fall down accidentally and hurt her. At first it was easy to keep her away. She had the puppies to look after and to play with on the grass. But then somebody came and said that a dog in one of the cottages near by, had come down with distemper. So, the next morning Dessi and Rosalinda took both puppies in town to get them vaccinated, and Little O was left without playmates for that day. Pysen had no time for her. He was handing tools to Papa at the new cottage, and that was much more fun.

So Little O got one of her "itchy" days, as Mamma used to say.

First she was in the way down at the new cottage, and they chased her out. Then she trotted home and with blue chalk began scribbling on Aunt Bella's white cupboards. She had already drawn quite a few figures before Mamma came and put a stop to that game. Next she sat down in a corner and began examining Knutte's new camera. Suddenly she had it apart. She didn't mean to, she only wanted to see where those nice pictures came from. Just then, Knutte came home to take a cool drink to the thirsty builders. He was so angry he was about to spank Little O. Mamma wouldn't let him do it, for Little O was so little and Knutte was so strong.

But Mamma did say: "Shame on you, Little O. You know very well that you are not supposed to touch Knutte's things. We shall have to send the camera to be repaired now, and take the money to pay for it out of your piggy bank. Go out and play now, instead of thinking up mischief."

Little O went outside. In the ditch she found a little frog, which she dropped in a newly filled jar of milk that Mamma had put on the table in the living room to carry down to the cellar. When Mamma scolded her and said that now she would have to throw away all that good milk, Little O asked why she had to do that, for the frog was awfully small and it was clean, too. Anyway, she only wanted to see if frogs could swim as well in milk as in water. But Mamma threw out the milk and freed the frog, and let it hop away in the grass where Little O couldn't find it, which was very annoying.

Then she went down to Lerviken, below "Ye Reste," where she and Pysen usually made clay figures. But instead of doing that she climbed down in the clay with her new red sandals. When she pulled them up again big lumps of clay stuck to the soles. That was funny, she thought, and climbed down again, stamping and splashing around for a while.

"Chipp, chipp," said her feet, and more and more clay fastened itself to the sandals.

"I have elephant feet now," she said in delight.

Sitting down on a stone, she saw the muddy water clear after her splashing. Then she watched stickle-backs and other small fish a while, took a look at Tanja the third, and old Rudolfina, so nice and newly varnished, lying at their buoys. When she finally stood up, the strong sun had dried the clay. She had light-gray clay stockings way up her legs, and the sandals were so covered with huge gray lumps of clay, you could hardly see them. She almost felt as clumsy as when she borrowed Mirre's big wooden shoes, the ones Mirre used when she was weeding the vegetable garden.

As she clamped up to the cottage, she sang the song Mirre used to sing:

> "Hi, Julia we go
> With wooden shoes, oho,
> Hi, Julia! Hi Julia!
> Hi, Julia, we go."

One can't exactly say that Mamma was very happy when she saw what her youngest one had done. She grasped her rather roughly by the arm, and marched her down to the water where she washed both youngster and sandals. She said she didn't think the sandals would ever be quite clean again. And she certainly wasn't going to get any new ones this summer, and a big girl like Little O really ought to have had better sense.

"You'll have to go barefoot today," said Mamma, "and if it hurts your feet, I am sure, you'll soon get used to it. Now, try to be good for a while. You were very naughty to ruin Knutte's camera. Why don't you go and pick some wild strawberries outside the fence and give them to him. He feels very down-hearted, poor boy."

Little O felt a little ashamed, and, as she thought more about it, she really felt terribly ashamed.

Because it was so early in the summer, the soles of her feet had not yet had time to get hardened. The grass pricked them and tickled uncomfortably. Walking gingerly on the edges of her feet she went out through the gate and began picking wild strawberries and threading them on a straw. Knutte was sure to be happy again when he got these. She didn't eat a single berry herself, although she was so tempted, her mouth watered. When she finished the long straw so that it looked like a very pretty red necklace, she went down to the cottage where Knutte stood handing nails to Lasse. She held the straw behind her back, and was just about to say: "I am sorry, Knutte, but guess what I have for you," when he turned around and angrily said: "Are you back again? You are a bad little girl, going around ruining things a person has worked and saved for. Didn't you hear what Papa said. You can't stay here. Now get going!"

"But I was only going to . . ." said Little O.

"Watch out, so you don't upset anything," called Lasse a little impatiently. "You had better go home to Mamma, Little O."

Just then Little O tripped over the box of nails, spilling them all. The nails fell down between the chinks in the half-finished floor. "Look what she is doing," cried Knutte. "She has upset the whole box of nails."

Pysen came running.

"Little O, you are a nuisance." he said.

And then came Papa and lifted her up.

"You are going to do as I say now," he said gravely. "I don't want you here. Now then, march on home with you."

Little O had scraped her knee when she fell over the box. The scratch on her knee hurt so the tears began running.

How mean they were to her. Here she came with wild strawberries for Knutte to make up with him, and all he did was to get angry and tattle on her. Then Lasse and Papa chased her away, although Mamma had said to go there with the strawberries. And her knee was smarting, and when she fell the strawberries got smashed and full of sawdust. And she never got to go any place where it was fun. She only had to get out of the way, so the others could have fun by themselves. And Truls and Pella weren't home yet! The big girls went off to the city with them, though they were her puppies. Nobody in the whole world was to be pitied more than Little O.

Well, she was going to show them all. She would go some place and hide, some place where they couldn't find her. Then they would miss her.

Knutte was surely not going to get any more wild strawberries from her.

Sniffling, Little O picked off most of the sawdust and stuffed the berries into her mouth. Then she threw away the straw and looked around for a hiding place.

For a while she sat down in the cellar. The cellar was like a cave under a hill with grass growing on top. It felt cool and good, smelling of smoked ham and fresh vegetables. From a bunch of carrots she helped herself to one, chewing on it for a while. It wasn't that it tasted so extra good on top of the strawberries, but she knew that she was not allowed to take anything from the cellar without asking for it. And if they thought she was so bad, she really would be bad! She considered taking a bite out of the ham, but it was hanging in a cloth bag and was too heavy to lift off the hook.

After a while her feet began to feel cold in the damp cellar. She had better find another hiding place.

She crept upstairs again. Had they come home from the new cottage and gone in to eat? Without calling her? Weren't they going to give her any food today?

She trotted down towards "Oron." No, it sounded as if they were still hammering and nailing down there.

A ladder that had been used at the new cottage was leaning against the big pear tree. It was a long ladder, and the top part was hidden in the crown of the tree. She had climbed ladders before, but, of course, never such a long one. Well, anyway, up there among the leaves and the small green pears, she was sure nobody would find her.

She began climbing. She had to take big steps for it was a long distance between the steps. Half-way up she stopped and looked down. It frightened her and she thought about going down again. Suppose she should fall!

But then she looked up. Just above the last step on the ladder the trunk had split in two. That would make a fine place to sit. She could stay there as long as she wanted. She climbed on, and finally, hot and tired, she reached the fork.

Holding on tightly she crawled in and made herself comfortable, leaning against the trunk and letting her feet dangle. The afternoon breeze cooled her cheeks and hair. Through the mass of green she could see Blueviken sparkle. She could see the top of Rudolfina's mast, too. This was fine! Let the others saw and pick up nails down there. This was much more fun.

She could not reach the pears. But she did not mind that so much, because it would take some time before they would taste like anything but dry pieces of wood.

A jingling, whirring sound came from the kitchen. What could Mamma be doing? It sounded as if she were whipping cream. Maybe they were having strawberries and cream for desert.

Somebody came from the new cottage. Little O craned her neck.

Papa. He must have seen her for he came straight towards the pear tree.

Little O held her breath and hid her head behind the trunk. There he was at the ladder. It creaked. Perhaps he was coming to get her down, and she wouldn't be allowed to sit in this beautiful tree any longer. They wouldn't let her stay any place!

When she stuck out her head again, thinking to call: "I don't want to come down," she saw that Papa had only come for the ladder. He was carrying it over to the new cottage where he placed it up against the roof.

How would she get down now?

Little O looked at the trunk. There was no place to get a foothold, at all. She couldn't climb down, and it was too far from the ground to dare to jump.

She was just about to open her mouth to call for help, when she remembered. She was going to show them she didn't care about them.

"Klingelingeling!"

It was Mamma ringing the old cow bell. Dinner!

The hammering stopped. Papa and Lundkvist from the shop and all three boys were coming up from the new cottage. They passed close by her pear tree, but nobody thought of looking up.

"Well, it will be good with a little food inside now," said Lundkvist from the shop.

Suddenly Little O felt very hungry.

"I think we are going to have meat balls," said Pysen pleased.

Pysen, who was only two years older than she, was allowed to go with Papa and build. But not Little O! "Away with you!" was all they ever said to her.

Suppose she called out: "Here I am. Come and get me down," they probably would start scolding again. No, she had better not call. They were mean, all of them. She would just sit here and starve.

Everybody disappeared into the house. But

Mamma came out on the front steps and began ringing the cow bell again.

"Little O-o! Dinner, Little O-o!" she called, and then she went in.

Little O sat silent and glum in the tree.

After a while Mamma came out again and called. And then all the others came, too, and began searching for her. They looked everywhere. It was just like playing hide-and-seek. They were down at Lerviken, and in the potato field and behind the house. And Mamma looked down in the cellar, so it was a good thing she wasn't there. They were getting more and more worried, and called and called. Little O had to hold her hand in front of her mouth to keep from answering.

"She was going out to pick wild strawberries for you, Knutte," she heard Mamma say.

"For me?" said Knutte, and now he really sounded surprised.

"Yes," said Mamma. "Take a look outside the fence. She couldn't have gone into the forest alone, could she? Yoo-hoo, Little O. Where are you, Little O?"

"Suppose she has fallen from the pier?" asked

LOUIS SLOBODKIN

Lasse anxiously, and he and Papa started running down there.

But that sounded too terrible to Little O, and she couldn't keep quiet any longer.

"Ho-ho," she sang softly.

She sounded like a cuckoo, a very little cuckoo.

"What was that?" Mamma stopped abruptly on her way out through the gate.

"I heard her," cried Papa. "Be quiet! Where are you, little one? Answer!"

"Darling, where are you?" called Mamma.

Yes, now it was "little one" and "darling." But they needn't think she had forgotten.

"I am here," she called.

"Look," said Knutte. "There she is, sitting up in the pear tree. HOW did she ever get up there?"

How they all stared!

"She must have flown," said Lundkvist from the shop.

"Climbed," laughed Little O. Oh, how she laughed.

"Impossible," said Lasse. "I can hardly get up there. How did you do it, Little O?"

"Climbed," she said again. "And I don't want to come down."

"Well, well," said Lundkvist from the shop, "she knows what she wants, that one."

"Dear child," cried Mamma frightened. "Hold on so you don't fall down, and we'll come and get you. Lasse, hurry! Although I don't see how you can manage to get her down."

"Why don't you want to come down?" asked Papa.

"Because you all were so mean to me," said Little O, beginning to sniffle and cry when she remembered how badly they had treated her.

"Say, she is sort of curled up at the edges," said Lundkvist from the shop.

"But, Little O . . ." began Mamma.

"No one meant to be mean to you," said Papa.

"Ye-es, they did, too," said Little O.

"Wait, I'll go and get a ladder," said Lasse.

"The ladder," said Papa. "Now I understand. The ladder was standing against the pear tree a while ago, when I went to get it. She must have climbed up, and was sitting there then, although I didn't see her. Why didn't you say anything, Little O?"

"Because you were mean. You chased me away,

when I only was going to give Knutte my wild straw-berries, a whole straw full," wept Little O.

"O-oh," was all Knutte said. "I didn't know that."

"No, you only were bad to me. But I have eaten up all the strawberries now," said Little O, wiping her eyes with a rather dirty little fist. "And then I scraped my knee so it is bleeding. Oh, how it hurts."

She had not noticed before how terribly it hurt.

"You poor little baby," said Mamma. "But here comes Lasse with the ladder. And now you can get down, and we'll all go in and eat dinner."

"Is it—is it strawberries? With whipped cream?" asked Little O.

"Yes," nodded Mamma.

Little O thought it over.

"Well," she said. "Maybe I'll come down then."

"Say, that settled it," said Lundkvist from the shop.

And then came Lasse and carried her down in his arms. That really felt dangerous. She had a ticklish feeling in her stomach, and she had to squeeze Lasse so hard.

When they got in Mamma washed her and put a band-aid on her knee. Then they ate meat balls with potatoes and salad, and for desert they had strawberries. And Knutte took the very largest strawberry from his plate and put it on Little O's plate, while Mamma gave her twice as much whipped cream as the others. And Little O ate and ate and ate.

Later on they all went down to the new cottage, and Papa gave her and Pysen a lot of left-over boards and said they could build their own house over by the gooseberry bushes.

Pysen and Little O kept on building all afternoon until evening came. Little O chatted and laughed and sang: "Hi, Julia, we go," so loudly that she even drowned out Miss Breemer's rooster, who stood crowing behind the fence before he drove his hens in for the night.

"Well, she is singing another tune now," said Lundkvist from the shop.

7. *Two Footballs*

One morning when Little O woke up, her face felt hot and stiff. And when she yawned she couldn't open her mouth all the way, because it hurt in the "hinges," as Pysen used to call the jaws.

"Dear child, how you look," said Mamma. "I think you must have the mumps. And in the middle of the summer, too."

Mamma touched her neck just below the ear.

"Does it hurt here?"

"Oh, yes," cried Little O.

"Well, I thought so," said Mamma.

"I am so warm I am burning up," said Little O. Mamma took her temperature.

"Yes, you have a little fever," she said. "That usually goes with mumps. But you don't have to worry. It isn't a bit dangerous, and it will be over in a few days."

Pysen sat up in bed and looked at Little O.

"Oh, such cheeks," he said. "You look like Knutte's football, only redder."

"I don't think I do," said Little O, peeved.

"Your cheeks really are quite swollen," said Mamma. "You'll have to stay in bed a while, that's all."

"Oh dear!" said Little O, ready to burst into tears. "We were going sailing in Rudolfina today."

"And stay on board tonight, and not come home before tomorrow," said Pysen.

"It can't be helped," said Mamma. "Little O will have to go sailing when she gets well again. It is a good thing the rest of you have had the mumps, so nobody needs to be afraid of catching them."

"Did I look like that?" asked Pysen, making a wry face.

"Of course you did . . ." said Mamma.

But then she began thinking.

"Or didn't you have them? No, I really think you are the only one who hasn't had the mumps. I think it will be safer for you to move down with the boys in 'Oron,' so you don't catch them, that is if you don't have them already."

"I don't want to be round like that," said Pysen. "Look how big her cheeks and neck are. She looks like Tomas Breemer."

Tomas was Miss Breemer's pig, and he was always hungry and always grunting for food.

"Silly Pysen, you are a pig yourself," cried Little O.

"She can't help it," said Mamma. "And you just wait, Pysen, you may soon be just like it. Wash thoroughly now and gargle with this. I'll air out your bedclothes and then we will move your bed down to the new cottage."

"Mamma, do I look like Tomas Breemer?" asked Little O.

"No," said Mamma. "Maybe just a little bit, though. But it will soon pass if you stay in bed nicely."

"Can I have a mirror? I want to look," said Little O.

She got the mirror and looked at herself in dismay.

"Such small eyes I have. And there isn't room in the mirror for my whole face, either."

Pysen was still hanging around. He couldn't decide to leave, for he thought Little O was so terribly funny to look at.

"See, this is the way you look," he said, blowing up his cheeks with all his might, and getting her to laugh. But then it began hurting. Little O cried out in real pain.

Mamma came with a soft roll and milk. But Little O couldn't eat anything. It hurt to chew and swallow, too, although Mamma softened the roll until it was mushy.

Later on Little O asked if she might have Truls and Pella in bed with her. But Mamma didn't think that was wise. Since Little O had a fever, she ought not play with animals.

Mamma chased away the reluctant Pysen. Then the girls came in to look at Little O. They laughed, a little, too, and Dessi promised to read to her as soon as she returned from the sailing trip. Rosalinda peeled an orange for her, and Papa patted her and said she was sweet anyway. Lundkvist from the shop peeked at her through the window and said: "You sure have got yourself fat and fine."

Lasse and Knutte also came visiting. Lasse sat down at the bed and whittled three tiny, tiny bark boats, no bigger than licorice boats one buys in the store. He used pins for masts and three-cornered pieces of paper for sails. And on a chair beside the bed he put a washbasin filled with water, so she could play with the boats from her bed. Everybody was so nice. Knutte let her have his flashlight, so she could stay under the covers and look at her toes to see if *they* had the mumps too and were big as potatoes. But they weren't. And Mamma gave her a cool rub with water and cologne, and it felt so good and cool that Little O said: "More, more."

Then Mamma had to go out in the kitchen to make sandwiches for the sailors, and they began getting together sweaters and waterproof jackets and started to carry things down to the boat.

Little O slept a little while, and when she woke up they were all gone. All except Mamma, and she was making jam in the kitchen. But as was always the case when they made jam, wasps would come in, and Mamma had to close the door so they wouldn't fly in the bedroom and sting Little O.

Everything seemed so sad and she felt so lonesome, especially when she thought of Rudolfina, now far out to sea with her brothers and sisters. She splashed a bit in the washbasin, so the little wooden boats would sail and bob in the waves. But even that wasn't fun for very long. Outside Truls and Pella were yelping. They were inside Little O's old play pen. Papa had built a higher fence so they couldn't jump over it. Nobody had time to play with them now.

"Silly, nasty, old mumps," said Little O. "How hot it is here. I want to go out. I want to play with my puppies. I want to go sailing and swimming. I don't want to lie here in this warm bed and have my 'hinges' hurt, and look like Tomas Breemer. I don't *want* to, I don't *want* to."

Angrily she kicked her feet against the foot of the bed. But she did not get less lonesome for banging her toes.

Then came Aunt Bella with the bus from the city.

"Darling, what's this I am hearing?" she said. "Lucky I brought this with me."

She took out a big thermos bottle filled with ice cream sticks.

"Here is something for you to lick on, little O,"

she said. "It will cool you off in the heat. I bought one for all of you, but since the others are gone, you can have all of them. They'll melt before Rudolfina gets back. She can eat ice cream, Maja, can't she?"

"I have always felt that ice cream was good for sick people," said Mamma, approvingly. "So far, none of my children has eaten enough ice cream to get sick on, although I am sure they have done their best to do it."

Little O licked the ice cream and enjoyed it. How wonderful it tasted and how cooling and good it was. Aunt Bella always knew what a person liked. And now she was good enough to sit by her bed, when everybody else had deserted her.

"Please, Aunt Bella, please tell about when I was little," she begged.

"You were terribly sweet," said Aunt Bella. "You looked like a little Eskimo child with your dark tuft of hair standing straight up, and your eyes looking like shiny black currants. A real little chatterbox you were. You would rattle off long, long strings of words, and you yourself probably didn't know what they all meant.

"Well, but later on, when I really could talk, what did I say, then?"

"I don't remember what were your first words. I think it must have been 'Mamma' and 'Papa'. But I remember when you were a little bigger, and were able to toddle around, you picked up all kinds of little creatures you found, and you would stand there holding them in your hand and talk to them. Do you know which ones you were especially fond of? The wood lice! You called them 'dood mice' and said they were sweet. I have never heard anyone say that they liked those loathsome little animals. But I suppose somebody ought to like them, too."

"I think their aunties like them," said Little O. "But I don't care much about them any longer. I like frogs now, they have such nice arms and legs, just like little children."

She put her hands up to her ears. "Oh, how it hurts when I talk."

"You mustn't talk so much," said Aunt Bella. "Eat your ice cream, and I will chat. Where was I now? Oh, yes, the green plant lice you liked, too. It was the pretty color, I suppose. We tried to teach you to say plant lice, but do you know what it turned out to be: 'ant mice.' Yes, 'ant mice.' You said that for a long time. And you chased butterflies, too, but you never caught any, of course. When you tried to say butterfly, it always became 'mutterfy', and the birds became 'mirds', and Mirre became 'mourteen' years old, you said."

Little O laughed merrily, thinking about how little and stupid she had been, and how much bigger she was now, and how much more she knew. But then she had to whimper a bit, because it hurt even to laugh. Mamma came in and gave her half an aspirin.

Aunt Bella went on talking about Little O, and what she did when she was little.

Soft, balmy air drifted in through the open window. Outside the cottage, the big birch tree with the gracefully hanging branches, murmured and rustled, and made Little O feel drowsy, when the wind combed through its millions of green leaves. In the middle of the story about how Papa and Mamma lost her the time they were on the Saucepan journey, the patient fell asleep. But she had heard it so many times before, it didn't matter too much.

She didn't wake up before the afternoon sun was shining straight in her face. And who but Pysen should be standing there in the sunlight, poking her cheeks!

"Are you home already?" she asked, and yawned. It hurt all the way up to her ear. "Aren't you going to sleep on Rudolfina?"

"The others are," said Pysen, "but they put me ashore."

"Why? Did you make too much noise?"

"Don't you see something?" asked Pysen.

And then she saw it. She had not noticed it before, because the sun had blinded her as she squinted against it, half-awake.

"Oh look, you've got the mumps, too," she cried.

"Mm," said Pysen.

"Oh, how funny you look!" said Little O. "You almost have as big a face as I have."

"Much bigger," said Pysen.

"Oh, no, I am the biggest one," said Little O. "I got the mumps first, so, of course, I am the biggest one, can't you see that?"

Pysen looked at himself in the mirror.

"I am just like two footballs," he said pleased. "I never have seen such a fat pig before, as I am, sick with the mumps. I am a really big pig, that's what I am! You are only a little marzipan pig beside me."

He always had to be the best of everything!

"Well, *you* don't have any fever. I have that!" tried Little O.

"Feel how hot I am," said Pysen. "Mamma said you only had ninety-eight and a half, and I am sure I must have over a hundred, at least. Oh—oh!"

"Do you hurt, too?" she asked sympathetically.

"Do I," said Pysen proudly. "It hurts so much I could go to pieces, tiny little pieces. But I don't cry!"

"I don't cry, either," said Little O. "I only say oh, sometimes; you have to do that."

"Yes, you have to do that," agreed Pysen.

"Mamma," called Little O. "Pysen says he is bigger than I am. Come look and see if I am not the biggest."

Mamma came in and looked.

"You are exactly alike," she said. "And you will both have to stay in bed a few days. Crawl into bed, Pysen."

"Is he going to stay in here?" asked Little O.

"Sure I want my two patients in the same place when I take care of them," said Mamma, and left.

"That's fine," said Pysen. "Then we can play the fox game. Where is the board?"

"Behind the curtain. Oh, are we going to have

fun!" said Little O, eagerly. "You can play with my boats as much as you like."

"First to be fox," said Pysen, throwing his tennis shoes under the bed.

"That's o.k. I would rather have the sheep," said Little O. "And Pysen! There is lots of ice cream in that thermos over there. Do you want some? If you turn it upside down and stick your tongue in, you can lick it."

"Mm," said Pysen.

8.   *Not a Pig*

It was a hot morning.

Little O crawled through the hole in the hedge with a bag of potato peelings and pea shells. She walked over to the pigsty to feed Mis Breemer's pig. The gate was open but the pigsty was empty.

In the pen with the dark brown pool in front of the pig's hut, there was no sign of Tomas, either. Only a little pink stone stuck up from the water, and an oak leaf was sailing around on top of the slimy surface.

"Tomas!" called Little O. "Tomas Breemer, where are you?"

Then the stone came alive. It rose out of the water, and she saw it was not a stone but the funny snout of the pig, the snout that looked like an electric outlet. Poor fat Tomas probably thought it was warm, too, since he had buried himself so far down in the mud to cool off.

Now he was peering at her with his small wise eyes.

"Come here, Tomas, and get some good food," coaxed Little O. Leaning over the pickets she emptied the bag while Tomas came rolling out of the pool, splashing and spattering mud.

"Oh, how muddy you are. It is terrible the way you have made yourself dirty," she said.

But Tomas didn't care one bit about what Little O thought. He went straight for the heap of peelings. "Slisk, slisk," said the soft little curled up tail, as he slung it against the slimy sides of his pen. He gobbled up all the good things in a few gulps, and when they were gone, he loudly grunted for more. Little O picked weeds and grass for him, which he swallowed just as willingly. Pigs eat everything, and Tomas Breemer could eat anything and go on eating night and day, if only he would be allowed to do it.

"Hello," called old Miss Breemer from "Ye

Reste." "Any of the Larsson children down there? Oh, it is you, Little O. Say would you be good enough to run an errand for me?"

Little O flew up the path.

"Oh yes," she called eagerly. "Where shall I go?"

"Do you think you could go to the bus and get a package? It is not heavy, but you will have to be careful, because it is a cake."

Of course, Little O wanted to go and get the cake.

"You see, Hilma is off today, and I am expecting guests," said Miss Breemer. "They are friends of friends, and are thinking about renting the 'Sea Cottage.' The lady is driving up in her car, and may be here any minute now. You had better hurry, for the bus will soon be at the corner. And come right back, please, for I want to serve coffee as soon as she comes."

Little O quickly started off. First she thought about taking the short cut through the pasture. But then she remembered that the cows were there this week, and one of them was dangerous. She had better take the usual road, even if it were twice as long.

Halfway to the corner she met a car. It was a

blue one with shiny chrome trimming. She had never seen such a fine car before.

A lady was sitting at the wheel. She stopped the car and leaned out.

She had merry brown eyes and dimples in her cheeks, and on the arm she held out towards Little O, she had a whole row of bracelets, and from all of them dangled small, shiny dingelidongs. Both she and the car sparkled and flashed, and Little O stared dazzled at all the finery.

"Hi there," said the lady, smiling very friendly. "This is the way to Miss Breemer's cottage, isn't it?"

Little O nodded.

"Yes, it is. Only we call her Miss Screamer. 'Cause she had an ear-trumpet before and we had to scream into it. Now she only has a button to hear with, and she doesn't hear so well anyway, but she is awfully nice, and likes children a lot. We always say that Miss Screamer is our nicest friend. We live in her apartment house in town, so we do know how awfully nice she is."

"Miss Screamer," somebody laughed from behind the lady.

And then Little O saw a boy, with a freckled face, protruding ears and lively brown eyes.

"Is that your boy?" asked Little O.

"Yes," said the lady, "it is. Don't you think we look alike?"

Yes, of course, anybody could see that, even if he was far from being as handsome as his Mamma. But he had the same merry expresion and friendly laughter.

"Hi!" said Little O.

"Hi," called the boy, grinning good-naturedly at her.

"Just drive the car straight ahead and then through the white gate," said Little O to the lady, and pointed like an experienced traffic policeman.

"Thank you," said the lady, starting the engine.

The boy turned and waved.

"I'll be coming soon, too," cried Little O. "I am only going to pick up a cake first."

She hurried up to the bus stop at the corner, and arrived just as the bus was leaving.

"Wait," she called. "I was going to get a cake for Miss Screamer."

"I put it over there, at the side of the road," answered the driver and started off.

Sure enough, there stood the carton. Little O lifted it up. It wasn't heavy. Could it be a cream cake? A fruit cake? For it could not be, could it, the very best of them all, a chocolate cake? Wonder if she would get to taste it?

But now the guests were already there, before the cake! Miss Screamer was probably impatient by now, waiting and waiting for Little O to come.

If only she dared go through the pasture, run quickly through it before that mean old Röllan noticed her.

She hesitated at the fence, but she didn't see any cows in there. They must have moved down to the sea, and were splashing around in the water, as they used to do sometimes when it was hot.

"I am going to do it," thought Little O. "I'll manage."

She pushed the carton with the cake under the fence, and started to climb over. It was easy enough to get up, but getting down was harder. Her dress caught on one of the posts, and it took some time to get it loose. Finally she had it off, although the dress had a little tear. Well, that couldn't be helped, that usually was what happened when she climbed fences.

Little O lifted up the carton again, and stole across the pasture. She was in such a hurry she didn't even stop to pick some huge blueberries she spied. For

Miss Screamer certainly had coffee ready by now, and maybe she would be standing on the porch looking for her.

She had just passed the big hazel bush when she stopped in alarm, her heart leaping into her mouth. There were the cows, and that mean Röllan was with them.

How frightened she got! She first thought about turning around and running back as fast as her legs would carry her, and then taking the usual road to "Ye Reste!" But then Miss Breemer certainly would be angry with her, and would think she just dawdled, because it would take so much longer. Instead she tried to sneak around the cows, stealing cautiously from bush to bush.

For a while it went all right. But you couldn't fool Röllan for long. Already she had caught sight of something moving among the bushes.

Röllan was a failure as a cow, Miss Breemer used to say. Her horns grew downwards, crooked and bent like the horns of a ram. "That's probably why she is so mean," said Miss Breemer.

Röllan slammed her feet on the ground and with her tail up, she came tearing after Little O.

"She is going to butt me," panted Little O.

LOUIS SLOBODKIN

The girl dashed on, and the angry cow after her. The other cows came jogging along, staring big-eyed at the race. There were no trees around to climb, only alder and hazel bushes. Little O ran in and out among them as fast as she could, but Röllan didn't let herself be fooled.

"Go away, mean old Röllan," squeeked Little O.

But cows have four legs and girls only two. So when poor Little O, worn out and trembling, took the chance of rushing straight for the backyard gate of "Ye Reste," Röllan quickly gained on her.

Little O ran for her life towards the red fence. If only the gate would be open! Her heart throbbed and her chest hurt. Behind her panted Röllan, and nearer and nearer she came. Never in her life had Little O been so frightened.

"Help," she screamed. "He-e-lp."

She was only a few yards from the gate when she stumbled over a tree root and fell flat on top of the cake. "Squash!" it said.

Now I am going to be butted to death, she thought. And already she imagined she could feel Röllan's crooked horns in her back.

"Mamma," she screamed. "Mamma!"

But what was this? No cow coming?

She picked herself up and looked around. There, not stirring at all, stood the dangerous Röllan, staring stupidly and amazed at her.

At that moment the gate flew up so hard the fence shook.

"Get in here, quick, before she starts butting you," called a voice, and the freckle-faced boy came rushing out with a long rake in his hand. "You hurry in, and I'll cover the retreat," he shouted and ran boldly towards the cow, swinging the rake.

Little O snatched up the carton, and flew in through the gate.

"Be careful," she cried. "Röllan is dangerous."

"Go away, you silly old cow," shouted the boy in shrill voice, chasing Röllan as if she were a little wasp.

At first it looked as if it might go wrong, and Röllan would attack Little O's defender. She lowered her head and glared in an ugly way. But then the boy let out a yell, a real hair-raising war whoop! To think that such a little boy could sound that blood-thirsty!

And then, just imagine! Röllan became frightened. Yes, she looked as if she had become almost wild with terror. First she stumbled backwards, almost falling down on her haunches. Then, slinging her head around, she turned and ran, through the pasture. Her terror spead to the other cows. They rushed off in full speed, every single one, and Little O behind the gate saw only tails and running feet until they disappeared among the bushes.

"That was an awfully good way to yell," said Little O, admiringly, to the boy.

"Oh, it was only an Indian war whoop," said the boy.

"But how did you dare? That cow is dangerous."

"Well if one isn't afraid . . ." said the boy.

"Yes, but she has hurt people," said Little O. "She butted the fisher's Ingeborg, so she had to go to the hospital."

"I don't think he is dangerous today," said the boy. "He stopped chasing you when he saw you falling."

"Do you say He about a cow?" asked Little O. "A cow is not a *He*. It is a *She*."

"Yes, I know that, of course, even if I did say it wrong," laughed the boy. "Well, aren't you going in with the cake?"

"I don't dare," said Little O, staring sadly at the flattened carton. "See, the cake got squashed when

I fell on it. What's Miss Screamer going to say? She told me to be careful with it."

"Oh, it is just as good, even if it is a little flat, isn't it?" he said. "Come on, I'll go with you."

He took hold of the string and between them they carried it in. And Little O didn't feel afraid any longer. But Miss Breemer looked in alarm at the carton.

"My nice cake," she said. "Yes, I thought, you were too little to run errands."

"No, she isn't," said the boy. "It was because of that old cow."

And then he began telling all about how Röllan had chased Little O.

"What is he saying?" asked Miss Breemer. "I don't understand what he says."

For it was as Little O had said. With or without a hearing aid, the old lady heard very poorly, especially when somebody was talking fast.

So the lady with the jingling bracelets had to explain. She spoke slowly and clearly, and Miss Breemer, watching her mouth, understood most of it.

"Oh, that might have turned out badly," said Miss Breemer, shaking her head.

Little O also helped to tell.

"And then this boy came and drove away Röllan with the rake, so she ran and she ran," she said.

And even that, Miss Breemer understood.

"That really was good. Well everything turned out all right then. I am certainly going to tell the Blombergs that they will have to keep that cow tied up. And you children had better not go through the pasture. Do you hear that, Little O! Now, let us have some coffee and fruit juice for the children."

She opened the carton. The cake really was squashed and half of it was sticking to the lid. But, after all, the way it looked, wasn't too important.

"Chocolate cake," sighed the boy and Little O at the same time, feeling very hungry.

Miss Breemer gave them each a tall glass of fruit juice, and a huge slice of cake.

"You two may sit out on the porch, so we can discuss things in peace," she said. "And thank you for helping, Little O. When you have finished eating, you may go out and play with Tomas."

Little O felt cheated. She had hoped that she would be invited to stay and play with this new boy.

"I don't want to play with Tomas, because he is so dirty," she said, sullenly.

"What are you saying?" said Miss Breemer. "Dirty, no, I don't think so. And that wasn't a nice thing to say, Little O."

Why wasn't it nice to say that dirty Tomas was dirty?

"Let me look at you," said the brown-eyed lady to the boy. "Well, your hands aren't so very clean. Go and wash them before you eat."

The boy turned to Little O. "What's the matter with you? What are you fussing about? You aren't so clean yourself. Your hands are just as dirty as mine, and look, you have grass spots on your dress."

"I think Little O needs to wash too," said Miss Breemer, "although I don't think it matters very much if the children once in a while skip washing while they are here in the country."

Little O couldn't imagine why there was so much talk about washing.

"Well, but Tomas can't play very well," she said stubbornly. "He only messes around and eats all the time."

"*I* do?" said the boy amazed.

"Not YOU," said Little O.

"But that's what you said I do."

"Tomas, I said, not you," answered Little O.

"But I *am* Tomas," said the boy.

Little O just stared at him.

"Tomas is a pig, don't you see," she said. "Isn't he, Miss Screamer?"

"Excuse me, I don't quite understand?" said Miss Breemer. "Why don't you want to wash?"

The brown-eyed lady was laughing now.

"Yes, Tomas certainly can be a pig, sometimes," she said. "But I am wondering if it isn't another kind of a pig this little girl is talking about."

"About Tomas Breemer, of course," said Little O. He is a really dirty pig, messing around in the mud all the time."

"Tomas Breemer," laughed the lady.

And then Miss Breemer was in on the fun, too.

"Yes," she said, "the Larsson children call my pig Tomas Breemer, and the rooster Don Juan Breemer, and even the turtle has a pet name. His name is Isaskar Breemer. I suppose they think I need a family. Well, Little O, so you thought I meant you to go out and play with the pig? No, you see, this boy is also called Tomas."

Little O said she hadn't known that Tomas could also be a boy's name.

"But now you know," said Miss Breemer, "and I think you two had better go and wash your hands anyway."

Tomas and Little O washed their hands in Miss Breemer's flowered wash basin.

"You know, I really was mad at you when you said that, and I still don't like you very much," said Tomas.

"But I didn't mean you," said Little O, "and you should see how dirty Tomas Breemer is. We'll go and look at him when we have eaten, and then you'll see."

"Hm," said Tomas. "You just wait, and I'll think up something, too."

"You aren't VERY angry with me, are you?" asked Little O, anxiously.

"Oh, I don't get so terribly angry with girls as small as you," said Tomas, who was a little bit taller than Little O. And at that he stretched himself, so as to become even taller.

They carried the plates with the cakes and the fruit juice out on the porch.

Just as Little O was about to put her spoon in the cake, Tomas whistled.

"Listen," he said. "Can you stand on the head of a nail and eat cake at the same time? If you can do that, you can have my cake, too."

"There aren't any nails here," said Little O.

"Look over there, as many as you want," said Tomas, pointing to a row of nails in the worn floor of the porch.

"Will they do?" asked Little O. "You mean that I can have your piece of cake, if I can do it?"

Tomas nodded. "That's what I mean."

"Of course, I can stand on my head," said Little O. "I have done that a thousand hundred million times. But I never have eaten cake at the same time."

"Try," said Tomas. "But you can only try once. And I haven't tasted my piece yet. You'll get it as soon as you have done it."

Little O chose a suitable nail just the right distance from the wall. She placed the plate with the cake beside it on the floor, and put her head down on the nail. Then she jumped up on her hands, her feet against the wall. But when she lifted one hand to take a spoonful of cake, she lost her balance and rolled down, her face smash in the cake.

"Mmmmm, it doesn't work," she said, trying to

lick off some of the chocolate and vanilla cream that covered her face. "You are just fooling, Tomas. You can't do it."

"I wasn't fooling," said Tomas. "Can I have your piece of cake if I can do it?"

"Yes, but you can't do it," said Little O. Still she was a little uneasy, that she might be without her cake.

"Now, look at me," said Tomas.

And he put his foot on a nail and began eating his cake.

"Now I am standing on the head of a nail, eating cake," he said.

"No you're not," said Little O. "You are eating cake, of course, but you aren't standing on your head, at all. Because you are standing on your feet, and that's that."

"Isn't this the head of a nail?" asked Tomas, with his toe pointing to the worn head of the nail. "And don't I stand on it?"

"O-o-oh," said Little O. "That's not hard."

It was a little disappointing to have to admit it was as Tomas had said.

"But you were cheating a little, though," she said.

"Just a little," said Tomas. "Not much."

"Are you going to eat my cake, now," she asked, close to tears.

For even if her piece of cake was somewhat messy, she thought she never had seen anything that looked so good.

"No, of course not. You can have it," said Tomas generously. "I wouldn't like to have a piece of cake that somebody had stuck her face in."

"O thank you," sighed Little O, relieved. Hurriedly she began eating the whole wonderful mess, for suppose he suddenly would feel sorry about it, and change his mind?

"Good cake," mumbled Tomas, digging into his own piece.

"Awfully good cake," said Little O with her mouth full. "I have a brother, called Pysen. The next time we have cake at home, I'll have some fun with him."

Miss Breemer came out and asked if they wanted some more, and, of course, they wanted more.

"When you finish, play together nicely, while we go down to look at 'The Sea Cottage,' " she said and left with Tomas's Mamma.

When Tomas and Little O had stuffed themselves

with another piece of cake, and had finished all the fruit juice, they ran down to Tomas Breemer, and watched him wallowing in the mudpool. The other Tomas had to admit that Tomas Breemer was a very dirty pig, and that it wasn't a bit strange she wouldn't play with such a creature.

Later on they climbed through the hole in the hedge, and picked gooseberries from the children's own bushes. Then Tomas met Knutte and Pysen and the puppies. They also had time to climb trees and play games, all of them, before Tomas's Mamma called him.

Little O went with him through the hole in the hedge.

"Does he have to leave?" she asked. "We are having so much fun."

"I don't want to go home," said Tomas. "Can't I stay here?"

"We are coming back next week," said his Mamma," for I have rented 'The Sea Cottage' for a whole month."

"Good!" cried Tomas.

"Oh, all the fun we are going to have then," said Little O.

She went with them to the car and waved good-bye. When the car disappeared down the road, she rushed home to Mamma.

"Can you imagine, Mamma, next week we will have another boy here. Aren't you glad?"

"Yes, terribly glad. But who is it?" wondered Mamma.

"His name is Tomas, and he is seven years old, and he can rake away mean cows," she said.

"Must be a remarkable boy," said Mamma.

"And you don't need to think he is dirty even if he has a name like a pig." said Little O.

"Even more remarkable," said Mamma. "I never have seen a seven year old boy who wasn't dirty."

"Well, I mean, not so terribly dirty, just a little bit. And do you know that he can yell so terribly loud. I don't think there could be anybody else who could yell that awfully, terribly loud."

"Yes, I believe I heard him," said Mamma. "Sotarn heard him, too, for he became so frightened that he ran and hid under the bed."

"That was an Indian war whoop, you see," said Little O proudly.

"I thought so," said Mamma.

"And he can stand on the head of a cake, and eat nails at the same time," said Little O.

"That is really something," said Mamma.

"Yes, isn't it?" said Little O delighted. "And can you imagine, *HE* wants to play with me."

"Just imagine," said Mamma.

9. *Little O's Happy Day*

The little house near the gooseberry bushes was just about finished. Pysen was a big and wise Papa in charge of the work. Little O alternately was helper and Mamma who came with fruit juice or coffee for her thirsty husband.

When she was a helper, Little O tried to talk in a deep voice like Lundkvist from the shop, and when she was Mamma, she talked in a high, sweet voice. Pysen growled in a deep voice all the time. He walked with long steps and went around with a little pipe hanging from a corner of his mouth. He had made it himself, whittled it from the handle of an old cracked bailer. It was supposed to be Papa Larsson's beloved pipe, but it didn't look exactly like it, of course.

Pysen ordered Little O around, sending her now here, now there. She obeyed with enthusiasm, and they both had fun. And when they began living in their house, Little O got more to decide. For everybody knows that mothers know more than fathers about keeping house. Pysen was told to hammer in the nails for the towels and the pot holder, which wasn't much bigger than a postage stamp. And then he had to fix a place for the flannel pig in one of the corners. She also wanted a dish in which to put the food for the pig. And she got that, too. It didn't much matter that the pig's dish was only an empty sardine can which Pysen had found on the rubbish pile.

Dessi had made the pig. It was pink flannel and stuffed with excelsior, and its eyes were small, light-blue, mother of pearl buttons, and it had a curly tail. It was exactly like a real pig, with a snout that looked like an electric outlet, and big ears.

Pysen didn't think it was very proper to have a

pig inside. But Little O said she wouldn't dare leave her dear pig outside, for then Truls and Pella would get hold of him, and that would be good-bye to the pig. Already they had torn off half of one of his ears, poor thing.

Little O, of course, had been to see Tomas, Miss Breemer's pig many times, so she knew exactly what pigs had to eat. She set out a mixture of sour milk, old bread crusts, and mashed potatoes, peelings and all, for the flannel pig. The food had been standing there untouched since yesterday, but Little O pretended that he ate and gobbled as pigs will do.

Flies began to gather around the potato mash.

"Look," said Little O, delighted. "There are flies here. Now you can see it is a real pigsty."

Then Papa Pysen and Mamma Little O squatted down on a sloping rock to make a set of dishes from which to eat. On the rubbish pile they had picked up pieces of old china, and now with a stone, they were cutting and fashioning them into small round plates and oblong platters. Once in a while they would pound too hard and the plates would break, but then they would just take another piece. There was plenty of broken china on the rubbish pile.

"Well, I guess we have enough, now," said Little

O, and began carrying in her new plates and setting the table on the margarine box which served for a table. Even if the plates were not as nice as the doll service she had in town, she was much more proud of the new ones, because they had made them themselves. It certainly wasn't everybody who could make dishes, oh, no!

"But now, you'll have to go and invent some knives and forks for us, Pysen . . . no, I mean Papa," she said.

Since Papa Larsson was an inventor, she thought that all Papas were inventors, and Pysen had nothing against that. As far as he was concerned, there were only three kinds of jobs worth anything: a chauffeur, a flier or an inventor. It was fun to play being a chauffeur and a flier, but to be an inventor was the best of all, because then you felt so grown up and wise, and you really thought you were somebody.

"I am going down to the shop, so hi, then," said Pysen.

"Papas must say 'good-bye, little one,' not hi," said Little O.

"Good-bye," growled Pysen and left.

He found a few small sticks in the woodshed and

shaped them a little with his scout knife which he had inherited from Knutte because the blade had a deep knick. Not much whittling was needed, and the sticks were ready as knives and forks.

Little O went shopping with her berry basket, the one Kalle Korint had made and Dessi had painted flowers on. The store was wherever she could find things which might be used for food. She bought all kinds of things, and then she went home and began preparing the meal.

The sorrel leaves were shaped exactly like the hearts in a waffle, so she had no trouble with them. The small round leaves on the red sedum, that grew on the rocks, looked just like the prettiest small sausages. From the flat big leaves of the green sedum she could get excellent flounders, and if she dipped them, first in water and then rolled them in sand, they looked as if they were fried. The juicy stems of the meadow sorrel made wonderful rhubarb desert, and a daisy became a delicious yellow cake with white paper decorations around. Yes, there was much one could make, if one was as good a cook as Little O.

A box which had contained shoe polish, served as a saucepan, and the lid, of course, was a frying pan. The stove was made from four bricks.

And when she wanted to chop spinach from some pig weed she had gathered, she called to Pysen that he would have to invent a board for her. That was done in one, two, three. He just took a board, about the right size, from one of the walls and handed it to her.

"Now the hole is a window," he said.

"Thank you, Little Papa! It isn't such a bad thing to be married to an inventor," said Little O, for she had heard Mamma say that many times.

Pysen straightened up and looked pleased.

"Klingelingeling, dinner is ready," sang Little O.

So they sat down, each on a brick, at the margarine box and ate with the stick knives and forks from the new plates. The waffles and the rhubarb desert they gulped down. The sausages slid down, too, although they didn't taste especially good. But the flounders and the cake and the spinach they just played with, and later on emptied in the flannel pig's dish.

"And now you must say: 'Thank you, dear Mamma, for a wonderful dinner,'" said Little O.

Pysen pretended he didn't hear it.

"I think I'll go down to the shop and invent something," he growled.

"Oh, what are you going to invent now?" wondered Little O.

"A rat trap that can catch a hundred rats a minute," he said.

"Oh good, dear Papa," said Little O. "You'll get lots of money for that, I think."

"A hundred millions," said Pysen nonchalantly, sticking the pipe in his mouth.

"What are you going to do with all the rats?"

"I think I'll give them to Sotarn and Aunt Bella's Persson," he said.

"They can't eat that many rats, and Persson only wants herring and ground meat," said Little O.

"Then I can throw them into the sea," growled Pysen.

"Then the whole Blueviken will be full of rats, and we can't go swimming there," pondered Little O.

Pysen thought about that for a while.

"I guess I don't care about any rat trap," he said. "Maybe I should go and invent a diving suit instead, so I could . . ."

Just then two big balls, one black, one white, came whirling in through the opening.

The puppies jumped up on Little O, wildly licking her, and wagging their tails so hard from joy, one might think they would get out of joint.

"Oh Truls, oh Pella, stop it! Who told you to come in here?" cried Little O. "Isn't it funny, though, they always want to stay with me. But I think they know I am their Mamma. Come to Mamma, funny little things. Come little darlings, and I'll let you stay in my lap."

But then Truls and Pella caught sight of the flannel pig, which they loved but were never allowed to play with.

"Wooff," they barked, hurling themselves on him.

And just when Little O succeeded in saving the pig, they discovered the dish with his food. Then there were shrill yelping and long drawn-out howls with many angry little barks when they were not permitted to gulp down that delicious dish. The wild commotion was heard all the way into the kitchen where Mamma was ironing.

"Is there something the matter with the puppies, Little O?" she called.

"They are just being silly," answered Little O.

"Did you remember to give them their milk?" asked Mamma.

"Yes, I fed them and gave them milk a long time

ago, but here they come anyway, trying to eat the flannel pig's food."

"Puppies are playful, just like children," said Mamma.

"Let's go out and have some fun with them," said Pysen.

And so the inventor, Pysen, and his wife, Little O, rolled around in the grass with the puppies, playing hide the ball and then ordinary hide-and-seek with them until Truls and Pella were both so tired they crawled into the shade under the gooseberry bushes and fell asleep.

"It's too bad we don't have a roof over our fine house," said Little O. "Suppose it starts raining! Please, can't you invent a roof, Papa?"

"Of course I can," said Pysen. "But we have used up all the wood, and Papa says we can't have any more until he sees if there will be and boards left over at the new cottage."

"Can't we use something else?" she said, not wanting to give up.

Pysen thought about it and looked around.

Yesterday Mamma and Dessi had washed rugs down at the beach, and had hung them up to dry on the lines under the trees. They were nice striped rag rugs which Mirre had woven when she took her course in weaving. Pysen went over and touched them. They were completely dry and smelled fresh and clean.

"We can use these for a roof," he said.

They pulled a couple of rugs off the line and tried to stretch them across the little house. They couldn't quite make it, because the rugs would droop in the middle and then slide down over the stove and the food for the pig.

"We don't care about making a roof," said Pysen finally. "It isn't going to rain, anyway. Let's play something else with the rugs."

"Couldn't we use them for tents?" asked Little O.

They tried making a tent, but it fell down because they didn't have anything to prop it up with.

"Oh," said Pysen, "I know. Why don't we play Arabians? You know, the people Lasse was reading about in that book."

"Yes, let's," cried Little O, clapping her hands.

"And the rugs will be our burnooses, you know, the big cloaks the Arabians wear. We'll ride on camels through the desert and rob the caravans of their treasures."

"Oh, good," cried Little O. "But we don't have any camels."

"Those can be our camels," said Pysen, pointing to the boards in the swings.

"Oh, yes," said Little O.

Wrapping themselves in the striped rugs, each one took a board for a camel and rode out to meet adventure in the desert.

Miss Breemer's little puffed-up dwarf rooster, Don Juan, came in through the hole in the fence leading all his hens towards the potato field where there were so many wonderful fat worms. Don Juan was an unbearable, conceited gentleman, and considered himself the greatest rooster in the world. He was mean and would peck at the children even when they gave him food. His unbelievably shrill cock-a-doodle-doo often woke the whole neighborhood at four o'clock in the morning.

"There comes a caravan," cried Pysen. "They are merchants from India, and they are bringing a thousand bags of gold and diamonds, and we are going to rob them."

The wild Arabians urged their camels forward with yells and screams, as they rushed towards the caravan at breakneck speed. The caravan hastily

scattered. The poor attacked merchants dashed around cackling desperately. The proud leader flew up in one of the palms of the desert—that is, the apple tree at the side of the cottage. And there he sat, stretching his neck, scolding and scolding, almost choking with rage.

Dessi was coming out of the cottage. Both camels riders stopped short when they saw she had on her bathing suit.

"My how much fun you are having today," she said.

"Oh yes," said Little O. "I have never had so much fun before. We are playing robbers with burnooses, you see and it's so much fun."

"Then I suppose you wouldn't want to go swimming. If you do, I have packed some lunch in the basket. I thought we might eat at the beach today."

"Go swimming," shrieked Little O and Pysen in chorus.

They jumped off their camels and threw their burnooses down on the grass.

"Race you to the beach! Who will be the first one in the water," cried Pysen.

"The first one gets a cookie," called Dessi.

And off they went, Pysen first, Little O a bit after

him, panting and puffing, and last came Dessi with the basket.

When Little O reached the water, Pysen was already about to crawl out of his pants which were held up with suspenders. She knew she wouldn't have time to get her sunsuit off before he would be in the water, so she ran right into the water, just the way she was and sat down with a splash.

"I am the first!" she called out.

"You are cheating," cried Pysen. "You have your clothes on."

"I was first anyway," said Little O, turning around on her stomach, since she already was wet.

But Dessi gave both of them a cookie, and hung the wet sunsuit up on the branch of an alder tree. Then they all three splashed around in the nice warm water. Dessi and Pysen swam around chasing each other, and Little O played crocodile and swam with her hands on the bottom.

Later she put on a cork belt and followed Dessi on a trip out to Rudolfina. Pysen came swimming after them, looking like a dinghy after a big boat. They climbed up the little ladder to Rudolfina's deck, and sunned themselves for a little while, drinking a bottle of lemonade which had been left when they were there last. Finally they felt hungry and swam back again.

But in the meantime a great deal had happened on land.

When Pysen called to Little O about racing, the puppies under the gooseberry bushes woke up. They sat up, yawned and shook themselves a little, and then they considered following the three children down to the water.

But suddenly they caught sight of Pysen's and Little O's deserted house, and they just had to go in and snoop around a bit. Truls, at once threw himself on the food, shoveling down sour milk, potatoes, flounders and daisy cakes. Everything went down. And Pella finally caught the beloved flannel pig. With a firm hold on his ear, she shook him back and forth, and if he had been a real pig, he would have been as dizzy as dizzy could be.

When Truls had finished his in-between-meal he, too, rushed at the pig. They tore and they pulled at both ends. They were growling and biting, feeling brave as lions, and the poor flannel pig was terribly mishandled.

Then Pella happened to let go. Truls grabbed

him and rushed out of the house with him. Down towards the beach he ran, with Pella after, of course.

At the edge of the water she caught up with him, and the tug-of-war began again, back and forth along the beach. And then began the big slaughter.

Truls and Pella had often had fun, but never had they had *such* a wonderful time. Here there was nobody to disturb them or to take away their toy.

They tore the flannel pig into a thousand pieces. Scraps of pink cloth were scattered all over the sand, and wads of excelsior were sailing out over Blueviken. Truls and Pella did not give up until everything, even the curl on the tail, had been chewed up.

Then Truls laid down comfortably in the sun and closed his eyes. But Pella kept running around sniffing the air. Suddenly she found the food basket standing between a couple of big stones. That was something for a little dog who liked to eat!

When Truls heard her wrestle with the basket, he pricked up his ears, then he stood up to see what little sister was up to.

Truls took off on the run just as Pella succeeded in pushing aside such silly and unnecessary things as a folded table cloth, some plates and glasses, and had begun scratching out roast veal sandwiches and cold pancakes with butter and sugar, her little brother came flying and landed right in the food basket.

And that was what Dessi, Pysen and Little O saw when they came close to land.

Pysen was so upset that he went under and swallowed water, although he already was in shallow water. Dessi looked at the puppies in dismay, but then she couldn't help but laugh. Little O shouted to her dogs to keep away from the food. But the puppies neither heard nor saw anything. They only ate, standing there with their little tails up in the air, heads and forelegs buried in the basket, and stuffing themselves to their hearts' content with the delicacies.

Pysen was the first one to reach them. He grasped a black and a white curly tail, and hauled both struggling criminals back away from the place of the crime. But they already had succeeded in putting away most of the picnic food, and what they had not eaten they had trampled on. Satisfied, and with fat stomachs they sat there, panting in the sun, legs apart, like a couple of frogs.

"Aren't you ashamed, you messy pigs," exclaimed Little O. "Shame on you!"

"They don't know any better," said Dessi.

"Oh, I am so hungry," cried Pysen. "I could eat both Truls and Pella."

He had to take the basket and run home to Mamma for more food. When he returned he brought only sausage sandwiches, buttermilk and gingerbread cookies.

"There weren't any more pancakes," he sighed.

But sausage sandwiches, buttermilk and gingerbread cookies are good to eat, especially after a long swim, when everybody is starved. So it did not take long before it was all gone.

Dessi was looking around.

"I can't understand why there should be so much trash around here," she said. "Where has it all come from?"

"Look," said Little O, "look at those pretty pink pieces of cloth that have floated ashore? I can use them for my dolls or for dust clothes in our new house."

Dessi picked up a little pink rag.

"It seems to me, I recognize it," said Dessi. "It can't possibly be . . ."

"The flannel pig!" burst out Pysen. "It must

have been the puppies who have been here. Sure, look there! Excelsior!"

"Have you torn my nice little pig to pieces, you meanies?" wailed Little O.

"Well, that's too bad," said Dessi, "but you'll have to look after your puppies better, and hide your toys, so they can't do a thing like this again."

"But, what's the matter with Truls? Look at what he is doing," cried Little O.

Truls was very sick—up came parts of pancakes and roast veal, potato peelings, daisy cakes, small wet pieces of cloth and wads of excelsior, and a little, light-blue button.

"The flannel pig's eye," said Little O.

"Well that's the way it goes, Truls," said Dessi. "He who evil does, evil reaps."

Now Pella also began getting sick. Both puppies whimpered and cried pitifully, and Little O felt sorry for them, for she had been sick like that, too, a couple of times, and it had been no fun.

"Poor little darlings thinking that flannel pigs are things to eat," she said, wiping their noses with a handful of grass. It's only because you are so silly and so small. But oh, my poor flannel pig! I never had such a nice toy animal as that. I love it so-o much."

"The puppies did, too," said Dessi, "only in another way."

"You don't have to eat it because you love it," said Little O.

"You do too," said Pysen. "Don't you love ice cream? And don't you eat as much ice cream as you can get? Don't you?"

"Ye-es," admitted Little O. "But I don't eat up my animals, I don't. Now I don't have any pig for my fine pigsty."

"Tomorrow, I'll make you a new one," said Dessi.

"One like it? Exactly like it? With blue eyes?"

"Yes, just like it. And a curly tail, I promise," said Dessi.

"Oh thank you," said Little O, "you are so nice. You can kiss me, if you want."

Dessi kissed her on both cheeks and right on the nose.

"That's enough," said Little O.

The puppies with their heads drooping, looked as if they could not understand what had happened to them. They had worried wrinkles in their foreheads and were still trembling a little.

"Oh, you poor little dears," cooed Little O. "I'll forgive you, 'cause you are nice anyway!"

When Truls and Pella heard the well-known friendly tone, their tails slowly began to wag again, and they crawled up in her lap, rolling themselves into one single ball.

"Look," said Little O, "they are coming to say they are sorry. Aren't they sweet? Oh, I am so happy, I am the happiest, happiest, happiest person in the whole world! Isn't it true that I am happy?"

"Of course you are happy, Little O," said Dessi.

Elementary Library
Lake George Central School
Lake George, N. Y.